OPERATION ARTEMIS

SUSAN HAYES

ABOUT THE BOOK

She's the sexiest woman he's ever seen...and his new assignment.

Kurt just got the worst mission of his life—investigate JAG officer Bobbi Castille. He wants to get to know the vivacious beauty better, but his plan was to wine and dine her, not scrutinize every aspect of her life. If she's the spy they're hunting, his life just got more complicated, and his heart might never recover.

She hates secrets—but she's keeping a big one.

Bobbi is on a classified mission to learn who is spying for the enemy, and she's running out of time. If she fails? It's just the stability of the galaxy that's at stake—no pressure.

She's not the only one after the spy. Nova Force's best are on the case, too, including Kurt. He's as sexy as sin and ranks higher than chocolate on her to-do list. When the enemy strikes, Bobbi and Kurt are thrown together on a mission only one of them is trained for, and a romance neither one of them expected...

Copyright © 2021 Susan Hayes

Operation Artemis (Book #4 of The Drift: Nova Force)

Cover Art: Mina Carter

Published by: Black Scroll Publications Ltd

ISBN: 978-1-988446-71-4

For my Mum and Dad, for supporting me even when they thought I was crazy. And for my best friend, Karen, for putting up with me when I was definitely nuts.
This book is also dedicated to Heidi and Jenn, for their tireless cheerleading, amazing friendship, and general shenanigans.

1

"Private Reddy. I'm going to ask you one question and I want an honest answer. Did you do it?" JAG officer Roberta Castille asked the soldier hunched on a stool across from her.

"No, ma'am. I mean, yes, but no."

"Which is it? Yes or no?" Bobbi leaned back in her chair and fixed her gaze on the young private. *Veth*. He was just a baby. She glanced down at the tablet in her hand. Twenty-one. Not as young as she'd thought. *When did I get old enough to see twenty-year-olds as kids?*

The man straightened on his stool and met her eyes. "No, ma'am. I did not do what I've been accused of."

She considered him for a moment. He was a scared, angry young man, which wasn't surprising given the charges he was facing. He was also telling her the truth, and there was clearly more to the story than the brief report she'd perused on her way over. "Alright."

He blew out a long breath, his stance softening slightly. "You believe me?"

"I believe there's more going on here than what I've read." She set the tablet down and gave the private a small smile. "I'd like to hear your side of the story."

"I don't want to be dishonorably discharged, ma'am. I'll take whatever punishment is required but not that."

That got her attention. "Who said anything about a discharge?"

"The officer who arrested me. He said I was done."

She picked up the tablet again and made a quick note. "Did he say anything else?"

Reddy was quiet for a long moment before answering. "He called me disloyal and said I should have remembered whose side I'm on."

And just like that, she had a good idea what was going on. This story played out repeatedly all over Astek Station. Too many soldiers were packed in with a civilian population who resented their presence. Tensions ran high, and both sides had their share of troublemakers. "Tell me what happened."

She listened, made notes, and asked questions as needed. By the time he was done, she had the beginnings of a defense planned and more concerns she needed to send up the chain of command. In the Interstellar Armed Forces, even small changes took time. But she had an inside track to the highest-ranking officer in the area and she was taking advantage of it to speed things along.

Reddy slumped back in his chair, as if telling the story had drained the last of the anger away and left him deflated. "So, that's what happened. They were harassing Irani—uh, the Torski girl."

"And how long have you two been dating?"

The look of panic on Reddy's face was almost comical. "Me? No, no. We're not dating. She's just someone... a friend."

"I take it her fathers don't know?"

"That we're friends?"

She didn't bother acknowledging the lie. It was the first one he'd told since he'd started talking. Now she'd seen him try it was clear he was a lousy liar and probably a terrible poker player, too.

The silence stretched out for several long seconds, and she wondered how long he'd hold out.

He blew out a breath and hung his head. "Okay. We're dating. And no, her family doesn't know."

"You should tell them. I've been to their establishment a few times. They're good beings. And you did protect their daughter from getting harassed. If I were you, I'd use that to your advantage."

"Maybe. But what if I'm discharged?"

"Were you off duty at the time?"

"Yes."

"Did you know the male you struck was an officer?"

"No. He wasn't in uniform, and he's not from my unit. I knew they were probably IAF because..." he gestured to his regulation haircut. "We all look alike."

That made her laugh. "Not all of us, but I see your point. Do you see mine?"

He frowned and then nodded. "You're saying that

my intent wasn't to deliberately punch a senior officer. I was just being a good citizen. Is that what you mean?"

"It is. And the MP who arrested you should have investigated their behavior, too. You're not going to be discharged, Private. In fact, once I've spoken to Irani and gotten her statement, I'll try to get the charges dropped. Until then, you keep out of trouble and don't talk to anyone about this unless I'm present. Clear?"

"Yes, ma'am!" His words came out crisper now, the fear replaced with something more becoming to a soldier.

"And, Reddy? A bit of personal advice. Once you're through this, you need to talk to Irani. Then go see her parents and tell them what's going on. I can't promise it will go the way you hope, but honesty is always the best policy. You always want to base your relationships on the truth."

He dropped his head and the tips of his ears darkened slightly. "It's not really a relationship yet."

She laughed and rose from her chair. "You stepped up and protected your girl from some jerks giving her a hard time, and you got arrested for it. You might not think it's a relationship, but Irani could have a very different opinion on that. You should ask her."

"I... okay. I will. Thank you, ma'am."

It took her another half an hour to arrange for her newest client to be released back to barracks and start rattling a few cages about the piss-poor quality of the report she'd been given. She threw in a few pointed remarks about a biased investigation and the comments made to Reddy. By the time she was done,

Bobbi was hopeful that Reddy would soon be a free man.

She checked the time. Interviewing Irani and any other witnesses she could find would have to wait until tomorrow. It was late evening now, and while that was an arbitrary distinction on a space station that ran twenty-four hours a day, her day was nearly done. It was time to go home, eat, and crawl into bed for a few hours. And a few hours was all she'd get. When Colonel Archer had asked her to take on a secret assignment trying to ferret out the mole in the IAF ranks, she'd been prepared for challenges. What she hadn't considered was that working two jobs meant eating and sleeping became luxuries that didn't fit well into her new schedule.

When this was done, she was booking a week-long stay on Plasia IV and doing nothing for the first three days but lying in bed and eating ice cream.

Kurt didn't want to be in the gym this late. Hell, he'd rather not be there at all, but it was a necessity. If he didn't work off his excess energy safely, he ran the risk of letting his temper get the better of him. He'd worked too long and far too hard to let that happen. So, the more stress he was under, the harder he worked out. Usually, that wasn't a problem. Lately, though, he'd spent more of his downtime in the gym than anywhere else, including his bed. The problem wasn't that their new assignment was on a tight deadline with high stakes. He was used to that. It was why he'd signed on with Nova Force in the first place.

He counted out another set of push-ups and then rested while the computer automatically turned up the gravity for his next set. No, the pressure wasn't what kept getting to him but the fact they were investigating people he knew. Every one of the suspected moles were IAF personnel. Some of them had been to his commander's wedding for *fraxx* sakes. The whole team was on edge, all of them bracing for the moment they learned which of their friends and fellow soldiers had betrayed them to the Gray Men, so named because they were a nameless, faceless cabal that hid in the shadows. Some of their number had created the cyborg project. Others had concocted pharmaceuticals designed to alter the minds and bodies of their employees. They were believed to be behind everything from assassinations to black site research labs where cyborgs were experimented on long after they were supposed to have been freed. Their spies were everywhere. No one knew what their endgame was. The stakes were high, the death toll rising, and everyone on Kurt's team knew they were running out of time.

That was his team's focus. Kurt had been assigned a secondary task. There was another list of possible suspects—one that most of the team didn't know about. Only two names were on it: Lieutenant Commander Roberta Castille and Colonel Scott Archer. Castille was a mystery. Archer was the highest-ranking officer in the sector. Kurt's job was to eliminate them as suspects, and so far, he hadn't been able to.

Both of them had read the mission file that had been leaked to the Gray Men. The colonel had given Roberta access to that information, which made no sense given she was JAG. Her duties barely intersected with Nova Force's at all. Then there were Bobbi's family ties. During an earlier mission they'd learned that a Dr. Oran Castille had been working for his grandmother as a corporate spy. Oran was Bobbi's cousin with many of the same connections, which was yet another reason to consider her a suspect.

Complicating matters was the fact that parts of both Archer and Bobbi's files were redacted or sealed for security reasons, and that lack of information made it next to impossible to figure out what connections they might have to the Gray Men and to each other.

Were they friends? Lovers? *Fraxx*, he really didn't want them to be lovers. He might not be able to make a move on the pretty JAG officer until the investigation was over, but that didn't mean he wanted images of her doing wild, naked things with Archer in his head either.

Normally he'd get Ensign Eric Erben, also known as Magi, to work his cyber magic and acquire the information he needed, but he couldn't do that this time. After getting caught breaking protocol and more than a few laws to make progress in their fight against the Gray Men, the ensign was under scrutiny and would be for quite some time. Since Kurt was the one who'd suggested Eric break the rules, there was no way he'd endanger the man's career by asking him to hack the colonel's files.

There was also the fact that Eric wasn't aware of the

second list. Only he, Dax, and Trinity knew about it, and they'd all agreed to keep it from the team. If things blew up, they'd have deniability. The others couldn't be held accountable for an investigation they knew nothing about. At least, that was the plan. The longer this went on, though, the more likely they were to figure it out.

He finished his last set of push-ups and got to his feet, his arms burning. He toweled off some of the sweat and grabbed a drink from the dispenser, chugging the water as he scanned the room and pondered what to do next.

The only equipment in use was the treadmill. Cris had been on it when he'd come in, and the team's medic had kept up a punishing pace the whole time Kurt had been there. That was unusual.

Instead of continuing his workout, Kurt grabbed a fresh towel and wandered over to the lieutenant. "Pro tip. If you're running away from your demons, it helps to get off the treadmill first."

Cris snorted. "There's no escaping my demons. I'm just trying to tire them out enough to grab a decent night's sleep."

Kurt draped the towel over the railing. "Long day?"

Cris slowed to a cool-down pace and mopped his face with the fresh towel. "Do we have any other kind?"

"Not often. Something particular on your mind?" He might not be able to solve his own problems, but helping the team with theirs was part of his job. In Cris's case, the problem usually had to do with his teammate, Aria. One day, those two would stop dancing around what everyone else already knew. They were made for each other.

"I've been hearing rumors."

"Which ones? This is a military base. There are at least fifty flying around at any given second. And for the record, I don't believe the one about our commander being pregnant. He just needs to spend more time in the gym."

Cris chuckled. "I hadn't heard that one."

Kurt stayed quiet, waiting for Cris to speak first. If this wasn't about Aria, what had him so worried?

"Medi-bots," the medic said at last. "There are whispers that we're all going to be injected with nanotech soon."

He'd heard some of those same theories, but he didn't see it happening. "I've been hearing those stories since my first days in boot camp. The corporations developed medi-bots years ago. If the IAF wanted to dose their soldiers with that kind of tech, they'd have done it by now."

"They didn't want it spreading into the population at large." Cris spread his hands. "But that shuttle has left the cargo bay now. Babies are being born with the nanotech already in their systems. Not to mention our new allies, the Vardarians, all carry a version of that tech in their blood." Cris frowned. "Even my little sister has medi-bots thanks to her cyborg husbands and the rebellion."

Kurt felt like he was missing something. "Okay, so, maybe it's coming sooner than I think. I still don't see the problem. Don't you trust the tech?"

"It's not the tech. It's what it means." Eric jerked a thumb at his chest. "I'm a medic. If we're all self-healing, what's my role on the team? The guy who gets coffee for everyone?"

"You make the best mochas on the ship. You have a real knack for optimal sprinkle distribution." Kurt raised a hand and rubbed his fingertips together. "It's a true talent."

"Will mochas be enough to keep me on the team?"

"No. The fact you're a talented investigator with years of experience will do that. And it's not like we're all going to be immune to blaster fire and explosions. *If* we get dosed with medi-bots, we'll still need a medic on staff. Or have you forgotten how many times your sister has patched up those crazy cyborg friends of hers?"

That made the other man laugh. "That's a good point. Sometimes I forget my baby sister is a talented doctor too. I keep thinking of her as being tiny, sticky, and annoying. I'll ask her to share what she can about that kind of treatment. She's the closest we have to a specialist on the subject."

"Do that. And don't worry about your place on the team. You're stuck with us. In fact, I'm going to need your help soon."

"Whatever you need."

"Great. Clear some time from tomorrow's schedule. You're giving me a crash course on how not to *fraxx* up while hobnobbing with corporate snobs and the upper echelons of society."

"How long do I have to impart my wealth of knowledge to you, my farm-born friend?"

"Two hours."

Cris winced. "Well, I do love a challenge. I think that's enough time to make sure you don't insult anyone or start a war."

"Ha-ha. Funny. It can't be that difficult."

"Oh, yes, it can. You're about to walk onto the galaxy's most polite battleground, where words are weapons, and loyalties change faster than the appetizer trays."

"Wonderful. I can't wait," he deadpanned.

"You'll be fine. If all else fails, just stand at attention and don't say a word. They'll assume you're part of Archer's protection detail and leave you alone."

"That would work?" If it were that easy, he'd imitate a statue all night to avoid small talk.

"Usually does. You're not high ranking enough to be of interest to most of these people. Archer and Halverson will be their focus. Not you."

"Hopefully that keeps Brigadier General Pain in Our Ass busy enough he stays out of our business."

Cris pitched his voice low despite the fact they were the only two people in the room. "Until then, we just keep investigating him and the others."

"Exactly." None of them were happy General Halverson had somehow managed to get an invitation to the gala. After he'd interfered in Operation Fury and somehow allowed their prime suspect to escape from his brig, Halverson was banned from interfering in any future Nova Force investigations. He wasn't supposed to be anywhere near this part of space. Hell, the man was on their list of potential spies, which was one more reason he'd been sent off to ride a desk somewhere far away from here.

Cris kept talking in low tones. "Do you think he's gone Gray? I mean, it makes sense. But if he has, he's not being very subtle about it."

"I don't think he knows the meaning of that word. If he did, he wouldn't be coming back here so soon. As much as I want it to be him…" Kurt trailed off.

"It would be too obvious," Cris agreed. "And nothing the Grays do is obvious. Whatever they're planning, it's part of a longer strategy. So he's a distraction. Maybe accidentally. Maybe not."

Kurt clapped him on the shoulder. "This is why you shouldn't be worried about your place on the team. Good thinking. It might just be him being an ass, but what if it's more than that? Check into his staff and anyone else in his immediate orbit. See if anything stands out. Dig into that aide of his, too. Clooney. We know he comes from money. Maybe he's got connections we need to investigate."

"Did you just reward me for my insight with more work?" Cris asked, his expression somewhere between bemused and incredulous.

"It's the Nova Force way."

"I'm starting to rethink my reluctance to leave the team. I could make a killing in the private sector."

"Too late. You've proven your worth and I'm telling Commander Rossi to keep you forever."

"Damn. Guess I better grab some sleep, then. Tomorrow is going to be a busy day." Cris powered down the treadmill, stepped off, and then turned to face him. "And since I'm still the team's medic, I'm advising you to get some sleep, too. The gala starts tomorrow, and you'll be expected to look your best. See you tomorrow."

Cris left, which meant Kurt had the gym to himself. *Perfect.*

He pulled on a pair of training gloves, holding his hands out until the nanotech-infused fabric adjusted to the correct fit as he walked over to the heavy bag and started throwing punches. He didn't plan on stopping until he was too tired to think, but no matter how hard he pushed himself, one thought kept buzzing around his brain. Bobbi Castille. Whose side was she on? What was she doing here? And why couldn't he get her out of his head?

2

Bobbi barely made it through her door before her comm unit beeped at her.

"If that's you telling me I have another client to see, I'm throwing you in the recycler," she grumbled and dropped into the nearest chair with a weary sigh.

The message was from Scott Archer. "Prepare for secure briefing."

She looked up at the ceiling and frowned. "How the hell did he know I was back in my rooms? He better not be tracking me. That would be ten kinds of creepy and inappropriate."

Still muttering, she got to her feet again and stalked over to her desk. First, she did a quick scan to ensure no listening devices were present, and then she dug out the privacy field generator the colonel had given her. She activated it, and air around her shimmered as the device came online. She enlarged the radius of the field to accommodate the colonel's presence and then placed the generator on her desk and sat down.

The paranoia and precautions all felt ridiculous to Bobbi, but Scott had insisted. She didn't like subterfuge or secrets, and lately she'd been up to her eyeballs in both.

She took a quick moment to straighten her uniform and compose herself and then sent a one-word reply. "Go."

A holographic projection of the colonel appeared across from her. He was dressed in a dark blue sweater she noted with amusement was almost the same exact shade as the IAF uniform they both wore. In fact, she'd never seen him in any other color. The man was a walking stereotype for all things career military.

He was seated in a richly upholstered chair, his blue eyes meeting hers with an intensity that made it hard to remember he wasn't actually in the room. His hair was more salt than pepper these days, and he didn't try to hide his weariness behind its usual mask of implacable authority.

"Hello, Bobbi. You were late getting in tonight."

She sat back in her chair and relaxed. If he was using her first name, this wasn't an official call.

"Hi. I was working. And you should not be tracking me. That's…" She sighed. "I don't like it."

"I know, but it's for your own safety."

She arched a brow. "And not at all related to your need to be in control at all times?"

He snorted and raised a hand in acknowledgment. "Alright. It's *mostly* about your safety. What kept you?"

"Things are worsening around the station. The pressure is building, and something is going to give soon." *Veth*. If Private Reddy hadn't stepped in, it might have blown up today, in fact.

He nodded. "I'm aware. But for now, I need every soldier stationed here. Once the gala is over, we'll make some changes."

"I'll send you over a report in the morning. You might need every warm body, but I can give you the names of at least three who need to be reassigned somewhere away from the civilian population of Astek station."

His blue eyes narrowed. "What happened?"

"The same thing that keeps happening. Our side. Their side. Innocents caught in the middle. This time, it was a couple of ours and a young female Torski resident. My latest client is currently up on charges for protecting her. The MP didn't even include the names of the other soldiers involved in the report I was given. I need to interview the *real* victim and then I'll forward the information on to you."

He nodded, but his brow was creased into a scowl. "Do you think they're part of a deeper problem?"

She'd asked herself that question more and more often these days. "I think some of our personnel are being influenced in ways that benefit the Gray Men's agenda, whatever the *fraxx* it is. Are they personally involved? I doubt it, but someone's putting ideas in their heads."

He grunted in agreement and reached for something, his hand vanishing as he moved past the range of the scanner. When his hand reappeared, he was holding a glass of what she knew would be cognac.

"Where are you right now?" she asked. "I know you don't keep liquor in your office."

He chuckled. "These days, I'm tempted to, but tonight, I'm on the *Bat*."

"That is still the most undignified name for a ship I've ever heard."

"The *Bat Out of Hell* is my ship, and I can call her what I like."

"It's your ship… that my mothers gifted to you. I still think you could have named it after at least one of them."

Scott cracked a rare smile. "Who says I didn't?"

"I'm telling them you said that."

He raised his glass in a toast. "By all means. They've said worse to me, especially since I seconded you to my secret project. I've heard from my sister more in the last few weeks than I have in the past two years."

Which was likely one of the reasons he was keeping tabs on her. He might be a colonel in one of the galaxy's finest militaries, but that wouldn't save him from her mothers' wrath if anything happened to her.

Scott took a sip from his glass and then fixed his gaze on her. "Anything new on that front?"

"The good news is I've eliminated more than half the names you gave me. The bad news is our biggest concerns are still on the list of suspected spies." She tapped a button on her comm unit and flicked an encrypted data file at the hologram.

His comms chimed confirmation of the transfer as she continued talking. "This would go quicker if I didn't have to do my actual job at all hours of the day and night. Not to mention I had to sit in on several briefings about the Gray Men. Nova Force really wanted me to have all the information so I could defend Ensign Erben from Halverson's accusations."

"That's dealt with now, though?" Scott asked.

"Yes," she waved a hand. "But that's not my point. I had to go to those briefings and pretend it was all new information because you've instructed me not to tell them anything. If I could compare notes with Rossi's team, we'd get this done faster."

"We've had this conversation before. My order stands. You are the only advantage I have right now, and I can't risk anyone learning why you're really here."

"Plus, they'd be insulted to find out you decided to investigate them all to ensure one of them wasn't the mole. Not to mention the fact you have me mirroring their investigation in case they missed something," she said.

"And that. But I needed to be sure of their loyalties before I made the offer. I believed I could trust them, but I had to be certain." He paused to take another drink. "Speaking of… have you made your decision?"

She'd been expecting this question, but that didn't stop the tiny chill that raced down her spine as she prepared to commit herself to her uncle's crazy plan.

"I have."

"And?"

"The answer is yes."

He nodded, and she could almost swear his expression flickered to relief for a moment. "Good. I made the same decision but didn't want to mention it until you made yours."

"So, you're going to be my boss for centuries?" She wrinkled her nose. "On second thought, I've changed my mind. No medi-bots for me."

"Ha-ha. Funny. I think I like it better when we're on the clock and you have to be polite to me." He fixed her with a look that reminded her of her mother. "Can I ask what made you agree to it?"

"In the short term, for protection. We're living in dangerous times, and once the Grays figure out what I'm trying to do, I'm going to be a target. The harder I am to kill, the higher my chances of surviving. Long term, I want to make the galaxy a better place. This way, I'll have more time to do it."

"You sound like Celeste."

"She'd say I sound like you, especially the bit about being a target." The mention of her mom's name gave Bobbi a pang of guilt. She hadn't been able to discuss this with either of them, and she didn't like it. Secrets were taking over her life.

"She's never going to forgive me for pointing you toward the Judge Advocate General's offices. Is she?"

"Probably not. But they had their chance to change my mind before I signed on."

"Given their careers, I can only imagine how that went."

"There were exhibits, presentations, and final arguments." Mama Juliana was a sitting judge on the Unified Galactic Supreme Court while Mama Celeste was a defense attorney. They had prepared their arguments and hit her with them over a two-day period. It had been a masterclass in the art of presenting a case, even though they'd failed to change her mind.

"Probably best they don't know what we're doing tomorrow. Hmm?"

"Tomorrow?" She hadn't expected to be dosed that quickly.

"We've got enemies who can digitize their consciousness and move between cloned bodies, a rogue AI that's actively interfering with our investigation, and spies in our ranks. The first doses are ready for distribution. You and I are at the top of the recipient list."

"What about Commander Rossi and his team?"

"Are you absolutely certain none of them are compromised?"

She leaned forward and met his eyes. "Yes."

He exhaled and then nodded. "Then I'll make the offer to them tomorrow afternoon."

"And then I can tell them the truth?" She'd hated lying to them. Most especially, she didn't want to keep lying to Lieutenant Commander Kurt Meyer. He was a smart, capable, and damned attractive man. He was also one of Nova Force's best interrogators, and the one most likely to notice she wasn't being entirely truthful. She'd avoided him since their one encounter where she'd been defending Ensign Erben against some trumped-up charges.

Scott raised his hand in a negating gesture. "Then, we'll see how they react to the news of the medi-bot injections."

"You don't trust my assessment that they're not compromised?"

"I do. They wouldn't be getting the offer otherwise. That doesn't mean I'm ready to read them in on the entire plan. The more people who know about it…"

She'd heard this line enough times she didn't need him to finish the sentence. He was right. Too much was at stake. But Rossi's team wasn't being used to their full potential right now. Worse, she had the sense they didn't trust her. She disliked that feeling. Hated being on the outside when the truth was that they were all on the same team. But she wasn't imagining the wary looks and carefully worded conversations whenever she'd been brought in for another briefing. They were guarded around her. Cautious. And they had reason to be. After all, she *was* lying to them.

Scott reviewed the data she'd sent, asking questions as he went. Less than a dozen names remained on the list of potential suspects. By tomorrow, she expected to eliminate several more. It had taken several weeks of exhaustive investigation to narrow it down this far, and she was almost out of time to whittle the list down further. Plus, her intuition kept telling her not to discount anyone else. Their enemy was devious. They'd also had months to put their assets into play. They were playing catch-up, which was why she was here, secretly running her own investigation. She needed to try and find out how badly the Interstellar Armed Forces had been compromised and how deep the corruption ran.

"I think that's everything," Scott said once he reached the end of her report. "I'll send a courier by your office tomorrow morning to deliver the medi-bots."

"No doctor?"

"Afraid not. Too many questions that way."

More secrets. The weight of them was starting to drag on her soul, and so was the sense of isolation that came with having to guard every word she said. She was used to going it alone. Given her family connections and the status Mama Juliana held in the legal world, Bobbi had learned early it was best not to rely on someone if you couldn't be sure of their motivations. But that didn't mean she liked always being on her own. "Alright. I'll send you that report once I've interviewed the victim. I want to be sure she has the support she needs and show her that despite appearances, the IAF cares about her wellbeing."

"Thank you." Scott pinched his chin. "Is it really that bad?"

"It is." She took a deep breath. "I'm sorry, Uncle Scott, but I'm going to be blunt. You need to ditch the uniform and go see for yourself. Even in the few weeks I've been here, things have gotten worse. From what I've seen, all the leadership around here believes that things will magically get better once everyone hears the big announcement."

"You are not the first person to mention that to me lately," he mused. "You don't think things will improve once they know about the new military station?"

"I think we're past that now. If the new station arrived next week and all the military personnel were transferred there immediately, maybe. But it will be months before that happens." She leaned toward him. "I don't believe we have that long before this all goes sideways."

Neither of them spoke for a long moment, but in the end, Scott nodded. "Alright. I'll make an effort to go and take a look for myself. I've got a friend who would be happy to drag me around the station and show me all the ways I've screwed up."

"Sounds like a good friend."

"She's a pain in my ass." Scott drained his glass. "I'm going to get some work done and then sleep."

"Just think, after tomorrow's injection, we'll both have more time to work."

"I'm more looking forward to being able to eat whatever I want without worrying about fitting into my uniform." He grinned. "You have no idea how much I've missed eating empty carbohydrates."

"So *that's* why you opted to get the nanotech! You just want to eat like a teenager again."

"If you mention that theory to anyone, I'll deny it."

"I wouldn't dream of it. Your reputation as a no-nonsense badass is safe with me." She waved. "Good night, Uncle Scott."

"Good night, Bobcat. Keep up the good work."

She closed the link and rose to stretch. She had intended to go to bed early and try to catch up on her sleep, but that wasn't going to happen now. Scott's news had energized her, and by morning, she wouldn't need much rest anyway. The nanotech would see to that.

Once injected, the medi-bots would give her several

hundred years of good health. Along with enhanced healing, endurance, and a metabolic rate that meant ice cream was about to become a staple of her diet.

None of that would help her unwind tonight, though. So she'd do the one thing that always helped clear her head. She needed to go for a run, and on a station as cramped as this one, there was only one way to do that—on a treadmill. Not her preferred way to exercise, but it would have to do. At least she didn't have to worry about the gym being crowded. At this time of night, the odds were good she'd be the only one there.

3

THE GYM WASN'T empty after all.

Bobbi had heard the wump-thump of a bass-heavy tune even in the locker room, so she knew she wouldn't be working out alone. What she hadn't expected was to discover the gym's other occupant was the one man she'd been doing her best to avoid—Kurt Meyer.

He had his back to her and was beating on a heavy bag like it had insulted his mother, but she didn't need to see his face to know it was him. No one else affected her the way he did, even when he didn't know she was there. He was intense, intelligent, and hotter than a supernova. Three damned good reasons to stay out of his orbit, though it hadn't stopped her thinking about what might have happened if things were different. He'd asked her out for a drink the first time they had met. In another reality, maybe she'd have said yes. If so, she was jealous of her alternate self, especially now she'd seen him stripped down and sweaty.

He'd tossed his shirt onto the floor at some point,

giving her a stunning view of his well-muscled body. It also gave her a chance to see the scars that crisscrossed his back. She knew about them. But knowing someone had survived a life-threatening beating at the hands of their grandfather and seeing the proof of it for herself were two different things.

Her fingers itched with a sudden need to touch him, trace each scarred line, and feel the heat of his skin against her hand. His slate-gray sweatpants sat low on his hips, and every kick he delivered to the bag made the fabric cling to his ass in ways that were probably illegal on some worlds. In fact, she *knew* they were.

She forced herself to move before he turned and saw her ogling him. Picking up a towel from the pile, she deliberately moved into his field of vision as she crossed over to an open area on the mats and started to stretch. He raised a hand in greeting, and she did the same. Neither of them spoke, but she could feel the weight of his gaze as she went through her warm-up routine. She kept herself turned away enough she wasn't looking at him, but she could still watch him out of the corner of her eye.

If she didn't know better, she'd suspect he was a cyborg. His blows were powerful enough to make the bag swing, and his speed was impressive—especially since he must have been at it for a while before she got there. He worked out the same way he did everything else—with absolute focus and total commitment. It was a damned attractive trait in a man, yet another thing she had to pretend she didn't know about him. *Veth*, she despised the need to lie to everyone, especially him.

Once she'd finished stretching, she should have claimed a treadmill and stayed as far from him as possible. That was the smart move. Yet somehow, she found herself heading toward him instead. She grabbed the bag to steady it, still not sure why she was there. The man was a highly trained interrogator, which meant he was a walking lie detector—one she'd been lying to since the day she arrived.

He didn't say a word for the next five minutes. Neither did she. She'd made the opening move by approaching him. The next one was his, and she'd be damned if she gave him the advantage by talking first.

"Haven't seen you in here before," he finally said.

"I usually come in earlier. Work ran late tonight." She leaned into the bag as he slammed it with another kick.

"I know the feeling. Seems like the whole station is working overtime right now."

Small talk. *Ugh.* Still, it was better than silence. "The party has everyone hopping. I noticed you've been tapped to attend as part of Colonel Archer's group. I'm in there too. Maybe we can grab that drink we discussed while we're smiling inanely and trying not to nod off during all the speeches?"

He stopped punching and peered around the bag at her, brows raised and a hint of a smile tugging at the corners of his mouth. "Is that your way of reminding me I never followed up on my offer?"

"That would be rude. I was just pointing out that there will be free drinks at this overblown display of wealth and ego, and we'll both be there anyway…"

He looked slightly pained. "We will. For days. I don't suppose you're familiar with these kinds of functions? I'm not."

"I've been to a few in my time." *A few dozen was more like it.* Mama Juliana's family had connections to some of the most powerful families in the galaxy, not to mention the fact she was a sitting judge on the Unified Galactic Supreme Court. Bobbi had avoided parties like the upcoming gala since she'd applied to law school. She'd wanted to put as much distance between her and her famous mother as she could. It hadn't been enough, which was why she'd changed course and become a JAG officer. It was easier to hide her relationship to her uncle than it was to erase nearly twenty years of photographic evidence she was Justice Juliana Castille's only child.

Kurt was silent for a long moment, watching her with an intensity that made her uneasy. *He knows that wasn't the whole truth.*

She wanted to fidget or look away, but she didn't. She wasn't as well trained as Kurt, but getting the truth out of someone was as important to her work as it was to his. She waited him out. Again.

He eventually nodded, but the smile had melted away. "Great. I have no idea what I'm doing. I'm just a farm boy with a gun. I'd appreciate it if you could save me from making any serious gaffes. I don't want to do anything to embarrass Colonel Archer."

"I'd be happy to, but I think you'll do fine. Most of the guests are there to impress each other, not us."

He nodded and squared up to the bag again, this

time positioned so he could still see her. His next words landed with the same impact as the punches he threw. "I know why I need to be there. I'm curious, though. How did you get roped into it?"

She had a split second to decide how to answer him. She went with a vague truth and hoped it was enough. "Colonel Archer and I have a history. He trusts me. Right now, that's a rare commodity around here."

"How long have you two known each other?" He made the question sound conversational, but she knew it wasn't.

"Some days it feels like forever. He has a way of taking up all the air in a room. You know what I mean?"

That earned her a snort of laughter. "I do."

"I'm trying to get him to make some changes around here. This whole station is a powder keg. If something isn't done to ease the pressure, it's going to pop soon."

The rhythm of his strikes slowed a bit. "What kind of changes?"

There were enough layers to his question to build a three-tiered cake with a double helping of whipped-up suspicion as the frosting.

"I'm sure you've noticed the friction between the civilian population and the military personnel. It's getting worse. In fact, it's the reason I worked late tonight." She went on to explain about her latest case, leaving out any identifying details but giving him enough of the story to demonstrate her point.

By the time she was done, he'd stopped working out. He just stood there with his arms crossed over his broad chest, his focus solely on her. "I didn't realize it was that bad. I haven't been outside the military areas in..." he frowned. "Apparently I need to get out more. It's been a few weeks."

She decided she could give him one gift. He could do more with the information than she ever could. "I think, maybe, this is the work of the Gray Men. Nothing overt, and I can't prove it, but since I got those briefings from some of your teammates, I've been looking for signs of interference. This could be their handiwork. They like to sow chaos and discord. Right? It's something they do to keep everyone off balance and make sure there are plenty of things to distract attention away from whatever their objective is. I think someone on this station is fostering animosity, creating factions and then stirring up trouble between them." She shrugged. "Or I might be jumping at shadows."

He scowled. "Maybe, but it's definitely worth checking into." His expression softened, and a ghost of a smile touched his lips. "Thank you."

"You're welcome." She smiled back at him. The tension between them was momentarily gone, replaced by something just as powerful and far more dangerous —attraction.

Kurt was more than a little tempted to walk over and pull Bobbi into his arms just to see if she felt the same way he did. The signs were there, but they were subtle and hard to read, just like everything else about her.

From her sultry curves to the wicked gleam in her

eyes, Bobbi Castille was as confounding as she was beautiful. It was making him crazy. After weeks of deliberately avoiding her, she not only walked in on him at the gym but went out of her way to be helpful. He briefly considered the possibility it was a setup but dismissed it as unlikely. Bobbi hadn't tried to start up a conversation. He'd been the one to do that, his curiosity getting the better of his common sense.

He'd been able to read her well enough to know their conversation was dusted with half-truths and omissions but no outright lies. Then she'd opened up about her workday, and every word she spoke was honest and sincere. While he was trying to fathom the change, she'd dropped a new lead about the Grays right into his lap. Either she was the best damned spy in the galaxy, or she was something else entirely.

As much as he wanted to give her the benefit of the doubt, he couldn't—not with the clock running out. "One day, I'd like to hear the story of how you got a Tier-4 Black security clearance. What's a JAG officer need with that kind of intel access?" He softened the question with a smile.

She didn't smile back. "It was for a case. I'm not allowed to say much. A black ops team went rogue and started picking their own targets. I'm sure you know what I'm talking about. It was all over the news for months. To do my job, I needed access to some very sensitive information."

He knew the case she was referring to. It had come up in his investigation. He should have made the connection between that case and her clearance. It made sense. What didn't make sense was why she *still* had it, but that wasn't a question he could ask. He'd pushed enough already, and she'd given him what felt like an honest answer. "That must have been a tough case."

"It was. I don't think I'll ever forget some of the things I learned, no matter how much I'd like to."

He heard the haunted tone buried beneath her words and recognized it immediately. "I know how you feel."

"And you likely lived through yours firsthand. My knowledge came from vids, photos, and reports."

He shook his head and took a half-step toward her before stopping himself. As much as he wanted to reach out, it couldn't happen. Not until he knew what her game was and whose team she was playing for. "I don't think our brains care where the nightmare fodder comes from. They still find a way to use it."

This time, she moved a little closer, pulling herself up short after taking a single step. "The nightmares..." She gave an involuntary shudder. "When I was a kid, a glass of warm milk and a hug was all it took to fix a bad dream. I miss those days."

"Yeah. Simpler times." Not that his childhood had been like that. His mother had tried her best, but his grandfather's presence had been a constant storm on the horizon of their lives. It wasn't something he talked about. He'd long since learned to pretend his life had been as ordinary as everyone else's. It was a lie he'd told so many times he could almost forget it wasn't true.

For a second, he thought he caught a flash of

sympathy in Bobbi's eyes, but it was gone before he could be sure. She'd seen his scars. It was the first thing most people noticed when they saw him shirtless, which was why he usually stayed clothed, but he'd thought he had the place to himself. Maybe she'd guessed his life hadn't been so simple growing up.

Or maybe she's read a dossier on me and knows everything because she's working for the enemy. Fraxx, he hated it when his paranoia made sense.

"I think I'm done for the night. The craziness starts in earnest tomorrow night, and I'm going to need some rest before I walk into that *chorzet* nest." He tapped the back of each glove and the fit loosened enough to let him take them off. "I appreciate the assist with the bag."

If she was surprised at his sudden announcement, she didn't show it. "No problem. I'm going to hit the treadmill and then grab some shuteye myself. I'll see you at the opening ceremony tomorrow night." She made a face. "I should get my dress uniform out and see if it still fits. Ice cream as a coping mechanism has some drawbacks."

"Yeah. But it works."

She smiled, a real smile that hit him like a punch to the chest. "So, maybe if drinks go well, we can escalate to ice cream on night two."

Why the hell did he have to be attracted to the only woman in the damned galaxy he couldn't have? "That…is an interesting proposal. Do you think they'll have ice cream at this thing?"

She laughed. "You didn't read your invitation. Did you? The second night is a buffet dinner with music and dancing. There will be tables full of desserts. I'm sure one of them will have ice cream. At least, I hope so."

Dinner? *Fraxx*. No one had mentioned dinner or dancing. He really needed to get some pointers from Cris tomorrow and maybe try to squeeze in a dancing lesson in the sim-pods. Not that he expected to be asked to dance, but Murphy's Law was a sneaky bastard. Better to be prepared.

His reply should have been neutral and noncommittal. What came out of his mouth was neither. Apparently, the logical side of his brain had ceded control to his id. "If there's ice cream, I'll meet you there. I'm sure my orders include protecting any and all frozen desserts from possible attack."

"Finally, a man who knows what's really important in life."

Her eyes lit up with humor, and once again he found himself tempted to pull her into his arms and taste her mouth. It was time to go before he did something that could upend his investigation...and possibly get him slapped. Though getting slapped wasn't nearly the deterrent it should have been. In fact, it took his brain down an entirely inappropriate path. *Definitely time to go.*

"Justice, liberty, and ice cream for all." He put some much-needed distance between them, grabbing his shirt from the mat before turning back to look at her. "Have a good night, Lieutenant Commander."

Her brow lifted at the use of her title. "You can call

me Bobbi. By this time tomorrow, I think we're both going to be tired of titles."

"Alright then, Bobbi. Call me Kurt or Sabre. I answer to both."

She nodded and then replied with an echo of his earlier words. "One day I'd like to hear the story of how you got that nickname."

"Fair enough. You told me your story. I'll tell you mine tomorrow while we're having that drink." It wasn't often anyone outside his team pushed back at him. The fact Bobbi did was yet another reason he wished things between them could be different. Maybe one day they could be.

"You have yourself a deal, Sabre." She nodded once and made for the treadmills that lined one wall of the gym. He allowed himself two full seconds to enjoy the view she offered and then headed for the locker room. He was tired enough to sleep now. If he was lucky, maybe he'd dream of Bobbi. She might be off limits in reality, but dreams weren't bound by the same rules. And for now, dreams were all he could have of her.

4

FOR SECURITY REASONS, Bobbi and the rest of Archer's party traveled together, or as close to it as could be managed given the realities of life on a space station. The transports had to be small to navigate the limited airspace available along the main concourses that crisscrossed the station.

They were broken up into smaller groups and assigned a transport, each vehicle already manned with a driver and an armed and alert escort. It was a stark reminder that they were all potential targets, and the risk would only increase when they entered the gala proper. It made the back of Bobbi's neck itch.

Tianna Astor, the new head of Astek Corporation, had brought together representatives from every species, corporation, and influential group in the galaxy for this event. According to all the press releases, she was trying to improve relations between the factions before the corporations went to war again, but Bobbi suspected there was more to it than that.

By hosting the party here, Tianna had gathered up every target on the Gray Men's list and placed them in a location already on the enemy's radar… light years away from civilized space. It had to be a trap. Her Uncle Scott would know, but he hadn't mentioned it to her. The man was holding his cards so close to his chest they were probably subdermal implants.

She hadn't spoken to him today even though they had exchanged information. Scott had sent her a heavily encrypted message informing her that Kurt's team was attempting to gain access to her sealed personnel files. It wasn't a surprise. But that confirmed it. They were investigating her. The knowledge stung.

She'd sent Scott an unencrypted copy of her report detailing the truth behind Private Reddy's arrest, along with the witness statement she'd taken from the real victim of yesterday's attack.

Irani was a soft-spoken Torski female who tried to downplay what had happened to her until Bobbi revealed that Private Reddy was the only one in custody. After that, the girl had been more forthcoming. By the time Irani had told her side of the story, her entire family was gathered around, hands on her shoulders, offering their silent support.

"You make sure that boy isn't punished for protecting our daughter," Tagor, one of the girl's fathers, said to her as she left.

"And tell him he is welcome here anytime he likes. And so are you. There is always a table at the *Dobra Brin* for friends," added one of her mothers. "And boyfriends!"

Bobbi had left Irani frantically denying that she had a boyfriend to a group of laughing mothers and frowning fathers. That was a side to poly families she hadn't considered—so many overprotective fathers to deal with. Her mothers hadn't been easy on her early boyfriends either, but at least there had only been two of them.

That visit had been the highlight of her day. The rest had been filled with work—both standard and secret. The medi-bot injector was delivered as promised, and she'd left it sitting on her desk for the better part of an hour before she was ready to open it.

Just thinking about it made her rub the side of her neck where she'd injected herself. For a life-changing moment, the whole thing had turned out to be rather anticlimactic. She'd expected to feel different somehow. But apart from the fact she felt fully rested despite a long day of work, she was exactly the same.

Her daydreaming came to an end as the transport she rode in set down in front of their destination. She exited with the others, trying to stop herself from looking for Kurt. He'd traveled with her uncle and General Halverson, a fate she was happy to have avoided.

She followed her uncle and the general inside, pausing at the entrance to take it all in. Astek's corporate headquarters had been transformed. The lobby ceiling was festooned with swaths of gold silk that shimmered and danced in the light of what looked like thousands of fairy lights. The lights must have been controlled by some sort of collective AI because they moved in unison, like flights of pixies dancing in ever-changing patterns.

Clusters of beings stood in the lobby, serving themselves from the wide assortment of foods and drinks imported from all over the galaxy. She moved past them, walking along a strip of dark red carpet that led them to the doors of the reception hall. The décor in here made the lobby look shabby.

Chandeliers of hand-spun glass in a myriad of colors hung from the ceiling. The tables were all real wood, as were the chairs placed in the various alcoves and nooks for those who wanted a place to meet away from the crush. Bobbi had been to enough of these events to know that most of those nooks would have sound dampeners in place to make conversation easier and eavesdropping difficult.

The air was as fresh as a spring day, and everywhere she looked, she saw the trappings of wealth and power. From the crystal glasses in every hand to the trays of delicacies from all across the galaxy, everything here was intended to remind the guests that their hostess had more money and influence than almost anyone else present. As power moves went, it was a doozy.

A hand touched her arm, and she turned to find Kurt standing beside her, his expression one of bemused awe. He looked incredible tonight. His dress uniform was so dark it was almost black, framing his broad shoulders and hard lines to perfection. His hair was freshly cut and carefully styled to hide the fact it was longer than regulation allowed.

He lowered his head to whisper near her ear. "I'm

afraid to touch anything in this place in case I break it. I swear even one of those cute little floating lights in the lobby costs more than I make in a year."

A server walked past with a tray loaded with canapes fresh from the kitchens, and she selected two, handing one to Kurt with a conspirator's wink. "Try this. If I'm not mistaken, it's worth more than either of us make in *three* years put together."

He eyed the appetizer with distrust. "What is it?"

She bit into hers and closed her eyes as the delicacy filled her mouth with a familiar popping sensation and the flavors of the sea. She took her time, enjoying the experience. When her mouth was empty, she smiled at him. "It's called caviar. It's delicious."

"That's not a lot to go on. What the hell is caviar?"

"Just trust me. Try it first. Then I'll tell you. It's really good."

"It can't be worse than the algae broth Fido—I mean Commander Rossi—made me eat once…" He closed his eyes and took a bite.

He didn't savor it the way she had, but he didn't blanch either. She should probably have warned him about the eggs bursting on contact… but it was more fun this way.

Kurt swallowed and opened his eyes. "Okay. That was…weird. What did I just eat?"

"One of the rarest delicacies in the galaxy. The only sturgeon alive today were transported off Earth in the last days before the Collapse. Though the fish are clones, their eggs have to be created naturally and harvested by hand."

His hazel eyes widened. "You fed me fish eggs?"

"Very expensive fish eggs," she confirmed with only a trace of a giggle.

"You could have warned me."

"Then you wouldn't have tried it." She popped the rest of her caviar into her mouth and uttered a soft moan of approval. "So good." She managed to murmur with her mouth still full.

A flash of heat sparked in his eyes as he heard her moan. "If this is how you react to caviar, I can't wait to see what happens when you eat ice cream."

His reaction made her cheeks heat. "Eat your caviar."

He did. "You were right. I wouldn't have tried it if I had known what it was. And it's actually pretty good."

"So, you trust me now?" She regretted the words the moment they left her lips. Of course he didn't. She was under investigation. He wouldn't trust her until he was sure she wasn't a threat.

The look he gave her was heavy with meaning…and entirely unreadable. Dammit. "No. But I think you knew that already."

"I suspected it, but thank you for being honest with me." She snagged a flute of champagne from a passing server and raised the glass to Kurt. "For the record, I *do* trust you."

His mask cracked, and she saw a flash of surprise in his eyes. "Thank you. I think."

"You're welcome." She took a long drink from her glass. With the medi-bots now in her system, she'd never get drunk again, but she could still enjoy the flavor.

"We should get back to work," he said a moment later.

This time, she didn't let him walk away first. Instead she smiled sweetly. "I never stopped. I'm going to mingle for a bit and try to bring over several of the guests for introductions to the colonel. I've already located two he wanted to meet tonight. I'll see you later for that drink."

She was already moving by the time he spoke again.

"Right. Good hunting."

"Same to you." And with that, she entered the fray and picked her first target—a Torski ambassador who stood half a meter taller than anyone else in the room. She knew the perfect way to strike up a conversation, too. One thing every species had in common—they always appreciated knowing where to find the tastes of home. Thanks to Private Reddy and Irani, she had her opening.

Shepherding guests to her uncle for introductions was only one of her tasks tonight. The other was to keep track of her remaining suspected spies and ensure they didn't do anything to endanger the guests, the peace, or the station. Now all she had to do was stay focused on those tasks instead of getting distracted by a certain sexy, suspicious blond who thought she might be a traitor. The fact he even suspected her proved that, as good as he was, Kurt Meyer still needed to learn a few things about reading people.

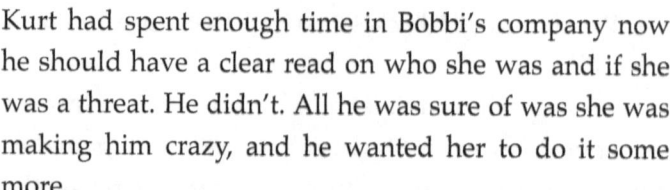

Kurt had spent enough time in Bobbi's company now he should have a clear read on who she was and if she was a threat. He didn't. All he was sure of was she was making him crazy, and he wanted her to do it some more.

As he watched her go, Trinity's voice sounded in his ear. "So *that's* why you're single."

"What?" he muttered under his breath.

"A smart, gorgeous woman just flirted with you, and you told her you don't trust her. Not exactly the smoothest move in the history of courtships."

"She's not available." Not until he found a way to clear her from his list of suspects, anyway.

There was a soft click in his ear, a sign Trinity had moved them to a private channel. "I don't think she's a traitor, and I don't think you do, either. What's your gut say, Sabre?" Trinity asked.

"It says she's clean. But my gut instinct isn't enough. Until I can prove it, she's off limits."

"True. But that doesn't mean you need to jettison any shot you have with her into the nearest black hole either. Clearly the woman has figured out she's on your radar in more ways than one, and she's still flirting. Take the hint, Sabre. She likes you. Don't screw it up."

He'd moved into the thick of the crowd now, which meant he couldn't answer, so he grunted in acknowledgment and shifted his focus to the major assignment for tonight. He was here to protect the colonel while keeping an eye on both Archer and Bobbi.

The rest of the team were positioned nearby, monitoring security feeds of the party. If they saw anything of interest, they'd let him know.

Ninety minutes later, he was more than ready to track down Bobbi and grab that drink. The rich and powerful's idea of a fun evening apparently involved a great deal of humble bragging, posturing, and small talk so littered with land mines and barbs it was a wonder no one was bleeding. At least Cris had been right. Most of the guests barely glanced his way. He was damn near invisible, which suited him fine.

Once the welcoming speeches were done, the guests were left to eat, drink, and mingle. That gave him plenty of opportunities to watch the crowd for anyone and anything of interest while still giving him time to think.

Along with his assigned duties for tonight, he was still turning over the offer Archer had made to the team today. Cris's gossip had turned out to be alarmingly accurate. The IAF *had* been working on a medi-bot formula for their troops, and the colonel had offered them the opportunity to take the treatment.

It had been a blunt, no-nonsense offer. If they accepted it, they'd outlive nearly everyone they knew, excluding partners and children, who would also be offered the nanotech. Any babies born to the women on the team would be born with the medi-bots. They'd also have to agree to extended contracts with the IAF, and a clause detailed they could be reactivated at any time, even after leaving the service.

Each of them had been sent a multi-page

document that explained the benefits and risks. The whole thing was so top secret the room had been scanned for listening devices before the briefing… which was ironic given the man presenting the information was currently being investigated as a possible spy.

The fact the IAF was even considering it meant they'd abandoned all hopes of keeping the technology contained. That genie was out of the bottle and it was never going back. All in all, it was a lot to process, and that was before he spent too much time thinking about whether he would accept the offer for himself.

On the one hand, it made sense to take it. If Archer had access, then if he were the spy, the Gray Men would already know about it and quite possibly have a sample. If that was the case, his team and all of the IAF would need every advantage they could find. On the other hand, he'd spent most of his life using physical exhaustion to control the Meyer family legacy—a violent temper he'd been on the receiving end of many times as a boy. If he took the upgrade, he'd have superhuman stamina and endurance. There would be no way to take the edge off, and that was unacceptable. He would never give in to the rage the way his grandfather had.

This time, she met his gaze and raised her hand in a subtle gesture that mimed raising a glass.

Hell yes.

He gave her a slight nod, and she flashed him a quick smile. He had to rein in the urge to smile back. They were working, after all.

He turned to the colonel. "Just going to head out for some air, sir. I won't be long."

Archer gave him the faintest of nods, and Kurt slipped away with a sigh of relief.

"Trin, I'm stepping out for a second. Keep an eye on the colonel and let me know if there's trouble."

"Will do." There was a brief pause and then Trinity added. "Good luck."

He followed Bobbi out into the lobby. It was cooler out here, and the soft light was soothing. They walked over to one of the beverage stations and laughed when they both bypassed all the fancy drinks and went straight to the pitchers of ice water.

"If that's all you're having, I think I still owe you a drink later," he said.

"This is just to rehydrate. I'll find something more interesting to sample in a moment. Then I can nurse it for the rest of the night and still look like I'm partaking."

"While still keeping your wits about you." He took a sip of his water. "I had no idea small talk was a full-contact sport until tonight."

"And this is just the opening act. Wait until tomorrow night. By then, they'll have had enough meetings and negotiations to hammer out alliances and goals."

"Charming."

"Be glad we're small fish in this pool. The predators won't bother us unless we annoy them."

She wasn't being entirely honest. Even if he didn't know who her mother was, it would be obvious by the way the other guests reacted to her that she was worthy of their notice.

"You're good at this." He waved his hand around at all the finery. "I've been watching you."

She raised a brow. "You have?"

Well, *fraxx*. That hadn't come out right. "Watching you work the room, that is. The farm I grew up on had cattle dogs. You remind me of them. Move in, cut your target from the herd, and get them moving toward your goal."

"Did you just compare me to a *dog*?" she quipped, laughing softly.

"Uh. Yeah. But a smart, capable one with a lot of skill and talent." He gave up and laughed. "Would it help if I also said they were nice looking?"

"It might. If you mean it."

He looked down at her smiling face, and a surge of desire washed over him, wiping out every filter he owned. "I meant it. You're a beautiful woman and a damned impressive one, too."

Her blue eyes widened and her smile became almost luminescent. "Thank you. And since we're being honest, I'd like to say that I—"

Whatever she was about to say was cut short by a new arrival, leaving Kurt frustrated and curious.

"Roberta Castille, I thought that was you! What brings you out to the far edge of civilization?"

Bobbi's smile shifted to an expression so polished and perfect he couldn't help but be impressed. Then, she turned toward the new arrival. "Hello, Tianna. It's been a long time. I'm here for the same reason you are. Work."

Tianna Astor, head of Astek Corp and one of the richest beings in the galaxy, gave a fluting laugh and then dropped her voice to a whisper. "It really is nice to see you, Bobbi."

"You too, Ti. You had me worried for a second there."

Tianna winked. "I'm still me, just playing the role expected of me... for now." She turned back to smile at the two men accompanying her. "These are my husbands, Royan and Owen. Guys, this is Bobbi Castille. She and I got dragged to a lot of the same parties when we were kids."

"It's Lieutenant Commander Castille when I'm working, but you're welcome to call me Bobbi. And this is Lieutenant Commander Meyer."

"Nice to meet you, Bobbi. Kurt! Didn't expect to see you here. Did you lose a coin toss?" Royan asked with a grin.

"Something like that."

Tianna nodded to him. "Hello, Lieutenant Commander. Nice to see you again." Then she turned to Bobbi. "If you need anything, let me know. Will you? I have to get back to work. I'll have Tink send you my contact information later."

"You still have Tink?" Bobbi exclaimed. "Really?"

"Oh yes." Tianna pointed up at the lights. "Who do you think is controlling them? She'll be delighted to see you again. We'll have to visit after this is all over."

They said their goodbyes, and not five seconds later, they were alone again.

"She hasn't changed. Still a force of nature." Then she cocked her head. "So, are we going to pretend you don't know how I know her?"

He decided to be honest. "We are not. Your mother is something of a legend, and her family connections are extensive. It makes sense you'd have some friends in this world. But now I've had a taste of high living, I can see why you made a different choice for yourself."

She gave him an amused look. "Still not ready to admit I'm under investigation?"

"I have no idea what you're talking about." He paused and then tapped at his earpiece, disabling the mic so he wouldn't be overheard by anyone on the team. "And even if I did, I couldn't say otherwise."

It wasn't the stupidest thing he'd ever done, but it was probably in the top ten. Still, Trinity had a point. His instincts all told him she wasn't a security threat. Unfortunately, his instincts also thought taking her to a secluded corner, burying his hands in her neatly braided hair, and kissing her senseless was a good idea. He might have judgment issues when it came to Bobbi Castille. But even if he was wrong, he hadn't given away anything she didn't already seem to know. His next question was going to be how the hell she knew she was being investigated, and he was damned sure he wasn't going to like the answer.

"I see." She kept her tone level but had a smile on her face as she watched him reactivate the mic.

Trinity's voice sounded in his ear, her words tight and clipped.

"I hate to interrupt whatever the hell you turned your mic off for, but you need to get back to Archer, *now*."

"On it." He glanced down at Bobbi. "There's trouble inside. You stay here until it's safe. Clear?"

He didn't wait for her to answer. He knew she'd stay put. JAG officers were highly skilled lawyers and legal advisors, but they weren't trained soldiers. She'd be safer out here.

As he ran back into the reception hall, he grudgingly acknowledged a new complication in his life. It didn't matter anymore whose side she was on. He needed to know she was safe. Was this how it had been for Dax and the others when they'd met the women in their lives? Was this why they had all lost their minds? He had a sinking suspicion it was. Well, *fraxx*.

5

BOBBI DIDN'T KNOW whether to be frustrated or relieved. Every time she and Kurt started to connect, they were invariably interrupted. On one hand, she was supposed to be keeping her distance from him. It ensured that she didn't give away too much with a poorly chosen word or indiscreet expression. On the other hand… she really wanted to enjoy all sorts of indiscretions with Lieutenant Commander Tall, Blond, and Broody.

She amended her last thought. He was tall, blond, and *bossy*. He'd ordered her to stay in the lobby like she was a subordinate when they were the same *fraxxing* rank.

"I don't think so," she muttered under her breath. The moment Kurt was through the door and out of sight, she set off after him. If there was trouble, she needed to know about it. Maybe one of her suspects had finally tipped their hand.

One advantage of letting Kurt charge on ahead was she could follow him instead of trying to spot her uncle through the throng. Kurt wasn't heading to where they'd last left the colonel. Instead, he was making for one of the alcoves on the far side of the room. No doubt whoever was on comms was telling him exactly where he needed to be. She envied him the support he had and the way the team worked together. She was on her own. While she understood why it had to be that way, it didn't make it any easier.

She was halfway across the room when she got her first glimpse of the problem.

Her uncle was inside one of the sound-dampened conversation nooks, but she didn't need to hear him to know something was wrong. His stormy expression and angry gestures made it clear he wasn't happy, and neither was the man he was speaking to.

She'd never seen the other man before, which meant he wasn't on her list of suspects, but something about the way he and Scott were arguing made her think they knew each other. The stranger was tall with dark hair and a beard touched with gray. He wore a tailored suit instead of a uniform, but the way he held himself and the gestures he used suggested a military background.

Kurt arrived at the colonel's side and snapped off a picture-perfect salute before saying something that made both men turn and glower at him. The sound dampeners made it impossible to know what he said, but a moment later the stranger snarled something and brusquely shouldered past Scott.

Bobbi used the distraction to scan the rest of the guests. General Halverson was huddled with his aide, both of them looking overly pleased. She'd have to warn her uncle about them... once he calmed down. Three other beings on her list were among the guests tonight, but none of them were doing anything of interest. Two were watching the scene with her uncle, and the third was leaning heavily against a far wall. Judging by his off-kilter stance, she assumed he'd had too much to drink and was not currently a threat to anything but his own liver.

She heard a small cry of dismay and the crystalline crash of glass breaking off to her left. She turned in time to see a young Pheran male scrambling to his feet, his legs and hands bleeding from where he'd fallen into the broken glass.

Another Pheran male, this one from the elite caste, towered over him, the far larger male's stripes so dark they looked almost black. He was almost apoplectic with outrage and fury, cursing at the server in Pheran as he cuffed and kicked him.

The server bowed his head, holding his bloody hands beneath his chin, palms up in the Pheran gesture of subservience. He made no attempt to block the blows raining down on him, not even when the attacker used his claws.

Bobbi charged toward the scene, throwing herself between the irate Pheran and his victim.

"Cease!" she snapped and then repeated the order in Pheran. She wasn't entirely fluent in all the dialects, but she could make herself understood.

"Out of the way, female. You do not understand our ways. This useless fool has caused me insult. He must be punished," he retorted in Galactic Standard.

She widened her stance, making it clear she was not moving. "You forget where you are. You are a guest here. By raising a hand to our host's employee, you have broken the laws of hospitality and brought dishonor on yourself and those you represent."

There was an uneasy hiss from one of the other Pherans present, and the rest of his party stepped back as if distancing themselves from what was occurring.

Adrenaline coursed through her, but she wasn't afraid. Thanks to the medi-bots, if he hit her, she would heal. His reputation wouldn't.

"But that *sooran-nah* ran into me. He touched me!"

"Did that happen?" she asked.

"I did run into him," the server confirmed, his voice shaking.

"On purpose?" Somehow, she doubted it. Even though the caste system was supposed to have been abolished, no member of the lower castes would take that kind of risk around a member of the *taryn-nah*, the elites of Pheran society.

"N-no. Someone pushed me. I stumbled, dropped the tray I was carrying, and fell into the broken glass."

"And there we have it. It was an accident."

The high caste male snarled and stepped closer to her. "I have been sullied and will take what is owed."

This close, she could smell the wine on his breath and see the subtle reddish tint around the edge of his silver eyes. *Veth.* He was drunk.

"You are a guest in this place," she reminded him, hoping to get through the alcoholic haze befuddling his brain. She was dimly aware of the crowd forming around them, drawn to this new drama like asteroids to a gravity well.

The male raised his hand, his claws extended. She tried to remember her hand-to-hand training, especially the bit about blocking attacks. It was all fuzzy, and some detached part of her mind made a note to sign up for a refresher course soon.

Time slowed as the Pheran lashed out, making it seem like her attempts to block the incoming blow couldn't possibly get into place fast enough... but they did.

For a moment, she thought it had been a glancing blow, but then time sped up again and the pain hit all at once.

She cried out but didn't move, locking her arms in place to stop herself from cradling the injured one against her chest. His claws had shredded fabric and flesh, and she belatedly remembered that while she would heal quickly, she could still feel pain. *Ow.*

There was an angry roar, a blur of blue and a flash of blond hair as someone slammed into the Pheran.

Kurt.

They hit the floor hard enough she felt the impact through her shoes. Kurt landed on top of the Pheran and managed to slam him bodily to the floor again as he pushed himself back to his feet. "You just attacked a member of the Intergalactic Armed Forces without provocation."

"She interfered. I have the right..." The Pheran's protestations came to a wheezing end as Kurt placed his foot on the male's chest.

"No. You don't. Not on this station. And *never* against a member of the IAF."

Kurt raised his head to look straight at her. "We protect our own."

A bolt of pure heat chased down her spine as her body reacted to his message—not what he said but the unspoken declaration in his eyes. *I will protect you.*

She'd been raised to be independent, to be strong enough to stand on her own no matter what came her way. That didn't stop her from wanting to bask in his gaze and the knowledge he was ready to defend her... even if she didn't need him to.

She wanted to go to him. To thank him for what he'd done. Hell, she just wanted to be close to him, but she couldn't.

The pain in her arm was already fading, and a quick glance at her hands told her the wounds were closing over. It was incredible. She could actually see the edges of the cuts start to draw together, but that meant Kurt might see it too, and that couldn't happen. She tucked her arms in close to her chest and flashed him a grateful smile instead.

Scott was barking orders somewhere behind her. "See to the Pheran. No, not him. The one bleeding."

Then he was at her side. "How serious are your injuries?"

"No medics needed, sir. It's minor and I've always been a fast healer," she replied, keeping her words vague in case they were overheard.

Scott shot her a look that could have frozen the heart of a star and his next words came out in a low, hard hiss. "You shouldn't have gotten involved. Low profile, remember?"

She answered in a tone so low no one would be able to hear her. "He was attacking an innocent being. If you wanted somebody who wouldn't step in and stop that sort of thing, you should have asked someone else to be your guest tonight. And for the record, sir. Low profile went out the airlock when you nearly got into a fist fight five minutes ago."

He scowled, but she noted a hint of amusement in his eyes. He was putting on a show of being angry for anyone watching, but she knew he wasn't. Well, not much. "Point taken. However, unlike you, I didn't actually get hit. Do you know how much paperwork this is going to entail?"

"Sorry."

He snorted, but the scowl didn't leave his face. "I know you better than that, Bobcat. You're not the least bit sorry."

By the time that brief exchange ended, Tianna had taken charge. The glass was being swept up by an army of bots, the Pheran's entire group was being escorted out, the injured server was being attended by a pair of medics, and Kurt was standing not far away with his arms folded and his gaze locked on her.

Scott looked from Kurt to her for a few seconds, one eyebrow quirking up for a brief moment before his expression settled back into a frown. "With me," he ordered and then walked over to Kurt.

"Lieutenant Commander Meyer, did you just assault one of the guests?"

Kurt came to attention, his eyes focused on something past the colonel's shoulder. "No, sir. I prevented him from continuing an attack on Lieutenant Commander Castille."

"And you felt the only way to do this was by physical force?"

Kurt nodded, the motion sharp and tight. "Yes, sir. I did."

"I'm not sure I agree with your assessment of the situation. I'll expect a complete statement and incident report from you first thing tomorrow morning. There will need to be a review. Understood?"

"Yes, sir."

Scott turned to look at her. "The same goes for you, Lieutenant Commander Castille."

"Yes, sir!" She knew most of this was for show. She hoped Kurt did, too.

"I think it's time we left. Castille, see the medics for something to clean up those cuts and then call for our transportation. Once we're back you will go to medical and get treatment. Meyer, round up the rest of our party and escort them outside. I'll pay my respects to our host."

"Yes, sir," she and Kurt answered in unison. They parted without speaking further.

They both had orders to follow, but she felt Kurt's eyes on her as she walked away. She wanted to say so many things to him, but they would have to wait.

She didn't regret what she'd done, but her uncle wasn't wrong. There were plenty of reasons why she shouldn't have gotten involved. If it complicated things with the investigation or with Kurt, so be it. It was still the right thing to do.

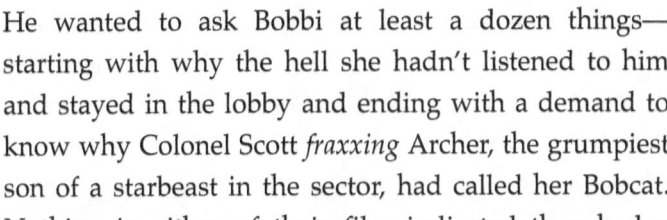

He wanted to ask Bobbi at least a dozen things—starting with why the hell she hadn't listened to him and stayed in the lobby and ending with a demand to know why Colonel Scott *fraxxing* Archer, the grumpiest son of a starbeast in the sector, had called her Bobcat. Nothing in either of their files indicated they had a relationship, but he could read lips well enough to be sure that's what he'd called her.

It made no sense. Were they just old friends? Former lovers... current ones? If she was with Archer, why the *fraxx* was she flirting with him? How did that fit with the possibility they were both compromised? He didn't believe that. She'd risked injury to protect someone tonight. Someone like that wouldn't work for the Grays. Not willingly. Could they have a means of controlling her? A family member held hostage? One of those explosive chips in her neck? His head hurt just thinking about it.

The first guests he tracked down were General Halverson and his aide.

"Sir. Colonel Archer and his party will be departing shortly. Will you be accompanying him?"

"Of course not. Colonel Archer needs to clean up his mess, but that is no reason for me to leave. We are here to forge new alliances and reaffirm old connections. That goal hasn't changed. At least not for me."

Clooney stepped in. "Sir. I will speak to some of your friends here and arrange for you to travel back with one of them."

Halverson nodded. "Thank you, Lieutenant Clooney."

"Of course, sir. I'll see to it right away."

Clooney left, and Kurt was tempted to check the floor to see if the man left a trail of slime behind as he slithered off.

Halverson shot him a pointed look. "Was there something else?"

"No, sir." Kurt heard the dismissal in the general's tone and left quickly. He'd only crossed paths with the man once before, and each meeting only made him more aware of how much he disliked him. Halverson was a self-important social climber who ignored all the responsibilities of his rank while embracing all the advantages it offered.

"Watch Halverson for the rest of the evening. And Clooney, too," he said, knowing Trinity would hear him.

"Already done. Trip's been digitally shadowing them all night." There was a brief pause, and then Trinity asked, "You don't look or sound happy. Something going on we need to know about?"

"Nothing urgent. Debrief later."

"Rossi wants you to make sure Archer gets back to base safely. And you may want to ditch the uniform before you meet up with us."

"Problem?"

"There's a rally happening on the main concourse.

Locals are unhappy about the party and the military presence."

"I'll make sure Archer is secure. Thanks for the heads up." He thought about the case Bobbi had told him about. The increasing contention between the station's residents and the IAF soldiers. As he walked through the elegant room, surrounded by well-dressed and well-fed people where even the air had been purified, he couldn't help but think the locals had reason to be unhappy.

He let the rest of the colonel's party know what was happening, and they all agreed to wrap things up and meet in the lobby in the next five minutes. Job done, he made his way out of the hall and spotted Bobbi in the corner. She was talking to something small and glowing. It was too big to be one of the lights, but it was definitely floating not far from her face. What the *fraxx* was it?

He stepped to one side of the door and watched. The whatever-it-was bobbed and spun, dazzling his eyes and making it impossible to get a good look at it. Bobbi was turned partially away from him, so he couldn't read her lips, and if he tried to get close, she'd see him.

"Trin. Cameras. Lobby. Castille. What is that glowing orb next to her?"

"Nyx is checking now. Please tell me you're not stalking her."

"Nope. Just curious about the bouncing ball of light she's currently chatting to."

"Ah. Mystery solved. Nyx says it's Tink."

"Tink? As in Tianna Astor's AI? It has a body?" Was that even legal?

"It's a hologram."

"Ah. Thanks. I wasn't sure what the hell I was looking at."

"No need to tackle the holographic fairy. Your pretty JAG officer is perfectly safe."

"Thanks for the tip. Since you have time to mock me, I take it you've already figured out who Archer was arguing with earlier. Is he a concern?"

"Too soon to tell. His name is Garrett Michaels. Ex-IAF. In fact, he's Archer's former XO from way the hell back."

Well, that was interesting in all sorts of headache-inducing ways. This operation kept getting more complicated.

"Any idea why he's here?"

Trinity sighed. "He's an invited guest. Apparently, he's one of the top corporate security consultants in the galaxy. We're still compiling a complete list, but he's worked for some of the biggest corporations out there. He doesn't appear to be too particular who employs him, so long as they can afford his fees. And looking at his yearly income? I'd like to suggest we consider going private for our next careers. I've always wanted to be rich enough to own my own planet."

"Please tell me you weren't being literal."

"He doesn't own a planet. But he could if he wanted to. Feel better now?"

"Not really."

"Me either. Oh, and you have incoming. Archer is

on his way out. If you need me, I'll be here, questioning my life choices."

"Don't let Dax hear you say that. I mean, we all wondered what you were thinking when you married him, but we didn't want to say anything."

Trinity was still laughing when Archer walked through the doors. Kurt fell in beside him.

"Sorry about the public dressing down back there."

"It was necessary. And I *did* tackle that Pheran asshole in the middle of the party."

"The asshole's name is Yvern Tesk, and he's being escorted off the station by Corp-Sec as we speak. Ms. Astor has also banned him from ever setting foot on any Astek property again."

"I'll include a formal letter of apology in my report so you can pass it on to her."

Archer nodded. "Good. It shouldn't be a problem, though. You didn't instigate that confrontation, and this isn't the first time Tesk has assaulted someone on the station. You recall that incident a few weeks ago when the Pheran doctor was taken?"

"I do." The Gray Men had kidnapped Xori Virness, a therapist who specialized in treating cyborgs. He and the rest of Team Three were involved in her rescue. They'd played a support role, mostly because the doctor's cyborg lovers had gotten there first. They'd already boarded the enemy vessel by the time the *Malora* arrived, leaving Nova Force to play catch up.

"Tesk was originally one of the suspects in her abduction. He assaulted her on the promenade because she accidently got in his way."

"And he's of the highest caste, so it had to be her fault. Just like tonight with that waiter. Of course, that whole caste system was supposedly abolished by their governments years ago." Kurt shrugged. "I guess no one told him."

Bobbi and several other members of the group moved to join them, and Kurt lapsed into silence. Tonight hadn't gone the way he'd hoped. There'd been no breakthroughs. They still had more questions than answers, and a lot of those questions were about the lovely and annoyingly mysterious Bobbi Castille.

She was walking a few paces away from him, her injured arm bandaged and held close to her side. As far as he was concerned, that was another of the night's failures. She'd gotten hurt, and he hadn't been there to stop it from happening.

She might be a suspect, but she was *his* suspect. Until he had proof she wasn't involved, she was his responsibility. At least, that's the rationale he was going with until he found a better one.

6

"You're grounding me? What about the investigation?" Bobbi asked incredulously. She was back in her quarters, talking to her uncle through their secured link. It was late, but Scott looked as fresh as he had when she'd last seen him a few hours ago. She wasn't tired either—another benefit of the medi-bot treatment. She was, however, angry enough to punch through the station's hull plating.

"Commander Rossi's team will see to that. Thanks to you, I'm confident none of them are compromised."

"So that's it? You brought me all the way out here to help you catch the spy, and now you're telling me I can't go to the one place where they're most likely to be so I can watch them."

"I brought you out here because I needed to know who I could trust. Thanks to your work, I know I can trust Rossi and his team. I know you wanted to continue the investigation, but after tonight..." He trailed off with a shrug.

"Will you let me at least talk to them? Brief them on what I know and who I suspect?"

He shook his head. "That isn't necessary. They're keeping me informed on their investigation. They've come to the same conclusions you have."

"So I'm not even allowed to tell them we were on the same team all this time? You told me yourself they're investigating me. They think I'm a suspect!"

"They think you're an unknown variable. That's all."

She glowered at him. "Since this whole conversation isn't officially happening, I am unofficially calling bullshit on everything you just said."

The bastard actually grinned. "Noted. And while we're off the record, I will tell you it wasn't entirely my choice to remove you from my entourage."

"Who else wanted me gone?" *Please don't say it was Kurt.*

"Halverson expressed *concern* about your behavior this evening. I haven't seen anything yet, but I'm expecting him to make trouble."

Well, *fraxx*. She should have known. "He's had it out for me since our first meeting when he was trying to destroy Ensign Erben's career. I wouldn't let him do that, so now he's out for payback. Is that it?"

"He's also hoping some of whatever he's about to sling at you sticks to me. After all, you were my guest, which means your actions reflect on me. He's a petty son of a bitch. Don't worry, it's not going far and I'll make sure the truth is known. You were protecting someone from attack. That's our damned job—a fact the general has forgotten."

"I'm still being punished, though."

"You need to stay out of Halverson's crosshairs. I need it to appear that what happened was properly addressed. I know you don't like it, Bobcat, but that's how it's going to be."

"Don't cross the streams," she muttered. Still angry, but it was fading to a dull roar now.

He blinked at her in confusion. "What streams?"

"Don't call me Bobcat when you're issuing orders. You can't be the colonel and my uncle at the same time. It's too confusing."

"Ah. Fair enough." He sat up straight, his expression hardening. "Lieutenant Commander Castille, you will not be attending the rest of the Astek gala as my guest. Do you understand?"

"Yes, sir."

"Good." He relaxed again. "You can tell him the truth once this event is over."

"Him? Who do you mean?"

Scott laughed. "Did you think I didn't notice? Give me some credit, please. Kurt Meyer barely took his eyes off you tonight, and I was concerned he was going to do that damned Pheran serious bodily harm after what he did to you."

She idly ran a hand over the spot where she'd been clawed. It was completely healed now, if a little tender. "Kurt would have done the same for anyone. Like he said, he was defending the IAF, not me personally."

"And if you believe that, I have some prime real

estate on Venus to sell you. As I said, you can tell him when the party is over. Your mothers would never forgive me if I did anything to jeopardize their chances of becoming grandmothers someday."

Bobbi hid behind her hands and groaned. "You did not just say that. We are not having this conversation. Uncle Scott, I love you, but that is a line you cannot cross again. Ever."

She lowered her hands. "Speaking of awkward topics of conversation, what happened tonight? Who were you fighting with?"

"Garrett Michaels is—was, a friend from another time. That was just a new round of an old argument." He waved a hand. "Nothing to do with the Grays or anything of import."

There was more to it than that. There was nothing *old* about her uncle's anger. That argument had been volatile, bordering on violence. "If you say so."

He changed topics, another sign he wasn't telling her everything. "I need to get back to work, and so do you. I'll expect a report on the incident with the Pheran in the morning, and you can send me a summary of what you saw and heard tonight that might be relevant to the investigation so I can point Rossi's team in the right direction if needed."

"Or you could let me continue—"

"Not an option."

"Yes, sir."

They ended the call and the hologram of her uncle shimmered and vanished like a mirage, leaving her alone in her quarters. She rose and padded over to the food dispenser, punching in an order for a hot fudge sundae with extra whipped cream. She needed to make a plan, and she had to do it fast. Her uncle had told her she wasn't coming as his guest. He'd never said she wasn't allowed to attend the gala as someone else's. She'd promised to meet Kurt by the dessert table tomorrow night, and she was going to keep her word.

If she happened to see anything of interest while she was there, she would follow up on it... on her own time, of course.

It had been a long, frustrating day for everyone on Team Three. They hadn't made any progress working out who the spy was. Only a few names remained on the team's list, including Halverson's. After Kurt and the others had left, the general had spent all his time glad-handing and spinning the events of the evening so it cast both Bobbi and Archer in the most unfavorable light he could manage. The man was a self-important asshole, but none of them really believed he was the spy. He was on the list because he fit all the criteria. Plus, they all hated him too much to strike his name off.

There were other issues too, undertones of unease that had no connection to the investigation. He wasn't the only one grappling with Archer's offer. The medibots came with a host of benefits, but everything had a cost. He caught snippets of hushed conversations about their options, and several of the team had taken time to chat with Nyx alone. As the only teammate already carrying medi-bots, she was their best source of information.

The only one who had already made up his mind was Eric. It made sense. He was engaged to Nyx. If he took the treatment, he'd have the same lifespan she did.

He'd done what he could to help. A private word with those who needed to talk. Encouraging those who were working through things on their own and keeping everyone on task as much as possible.

It was early afternoon when Dax tapped him on the shoulder and motioned for him to follow, leaving the others to their work.

"What do you need?" Kurt asked once they were out of earshot.

Dax shot him an amused look as he opened his office door. "I was going to ask you the same thing."

Once they were seated, Kurt answered. "I'm good. Trip says I'm ready for the party and shouldn't embarrass the uniform. Trin and I will do a comms check before I head out. Archer got me a special dispensation to carry a sidearm tonight. Concealed, of course, but if things go sideways, I'll be prepared."

"That's not what I meant. You've been busy helping everyone else process the whole medi-bots thing, but I haven't heard a word about how *you* feel about it."

Kurt shrugged. "It's an interesting offer."

"That's not an answer." Dax leaned forward. "This isn't an interrogation. Hell, it's not even on the record. This is me asking my friend if he needs to talk."

He almost said no. Almost. "Maybe I do."

Dax just nodded, waiting.

"You know what I can be like. I'm worried if I do this, I'm going to have trouble controlling my temper."

"That hasn't been an issue in years. When was the last time you were in a bar fight? Boot camp?"

Kurt rubbed the back of his neck. "Yeah. The one that nearly got me tossed out on my ass."

"That was the night Travis gave you your nickname." Dax grinned. He'd been there for that fight. There had been three of them back then. Travis, Dax, and him. Trinity's big brother was gone now, killed in action years ago.

"I'm just thankful only the Sabre part stuck. For a while there I thought I'd be stuck with Rattler for the rest of my life. And you know how I feel about snakes."

"I still think that was part of Trav's plan. After he saw you blast that rock serpent to ashes, he had your number." Dax leaned back in his chair until it creaked. Then he sighed. "I miss him."

"Me, too. If he were here, maybe we'd have found the damned spy by now."

"Or he'd be too busy kicking my ass for marrying his little sister to care about the investigation at all."

Kurt chuckled. "Or that. Though I think he's happy for the two of you. I mean, someone needs to keep your ass in line. He's gone and you outrank me, so it had to be Trinity."

"I'm good with that. But I'm also aware you're changing the subject. Medi-bots. You really think they'd be a problem?"

"I think they might be, and once I have them, there's no going back." His hands clenched into fists. "I've spent too long figuring out ways to not turn into my grandfather to *fraxx* up now."

"You want my advice?" Dax asked.

"No. But I'm betting I'm going to hear it anyway."

"Yep, you are. I've known you a long time. I've heard all the stories about your grandfather, your dad, and the legendary Meyer temper. Your grandfather was a certifiable asshole. Your dad was raised by said asshole, so of course he had some of the same issues, but he was working on ways to be a better man."

"And?"

"How old was your dad when he died?"

That wasn't the question Kurt had expected. It took him a moment to answer. "He was twenty-four."

"He died young. So young he hadn't learned how to rein in his temper. You have. You work out so much because you think you have to, but honestly, when was the last time you lost control?"

Kurt made a wry face. "You know the answer to that. Last night with Tesk."

"No."

"Did you somehow miss the part where I tackled him?"

"I didn't. You stopped him from hurting someone you care about, and then you walked away. You never lost control. If you had, he'd be nothing but a stain on that very expensive carpet."

"I… wait. Someone I care about? Castille? No! She's a suspect."

"You told me just this morning you didn't think she was involved. That you couldn't prove it, but your gut told you neither Archer nor her were working for the Grays. And I've never seen you tackle someone to protect a suspect before."

"Even if I had cleared her—which I haven't yet— dating someone after investigating them would be messy and..." he trailed off as Dax gave him a flat look.

"Would be messy and what? Please continue."

Kurt clamped his lips shut and shook his head. "Nuh-uh."

"Afraid I'll tell Trinity what you said? You know, given that's how we ended up married, she might have an opinion about your opinion."

"I'm sure she would. But since I'm the one who stepped in and set her straight when she was convinced you were a total bastard, I'm hoping you're going to keep my foot-in-mouth moment to yourself."

"That... is a good point. I owe you for that. I won't tell her."

"Appreciate it. You and Trin were different, though. You two already had a history. Bobbi barely knows anything about me. Other than the fact I'm investigating her."

"There's a way to fix that, you know. It's called talking."

"Hey, Bobbi, lets grab that drink and I can tell you all about the time I spent trolling through the minutia of your life." He scoffed. "I don't see that going well."

"I meant just talk to her. You know, like normal people do. Get to know her and let her get to know you. And since she seems to know and isn't glaring daggers at you from across the room, I think it's a safe bet she's going to forgive you. Eventually."

"Unless I'm wrong and she's playing me for a fool."

"I'll back your hunches over most people's facts. Besides, she's got a higher security clearance than either one of us. We can assume she's not using you for information, so it's safe for you to grab a drink with her."

"Or ice cream."

Dax cocked his head. "Uh. Okay. Or ice cream. Kind of old-fashioned for a first date, but sure."

"No, I mean, I can talk to her tonight over ice cream. We've got a standing date to meet at the dessert table."

To his credit, Dax did a passable job of hiding his reaction. It was barely more than a twitch of his brow and the slightest widening of his eyes. But to Kurt, it was obvious.

"What?"

"There's been a change of plans. Castille won't be there. Didn't you check your messages?"

"I've been a little busy. What happened? Is Bobbi too injured to attend?" He hadn't been fast enough. If he'd left Archer's side a few seconds sooner, she wouldn't have gotten hurt.

"No, she's fine. At least, I assume she is. Archer struck her name from his list of guests for the rest of the gala."

"Why? Is he punishing her for the Pheran thing? I'm the one who tackled him." He replayed something the colonel had said last night. *You weren't the one who instigated that confrontation.* Well, fraxx.

"Looks that way. And we know Halverson was playing up the whole thing after you left. Archer might be trying to protect her from the fallout."

"Knowing the colonel? It's probably a little of both." Disappointment and relief hit at the same time. Kurt hadn't realized how much he'd been looking forward to seeing Bobbi tonight, but it also meant she'd be far safer. Every analysis they ran indicated that tonight was the most likely time for the Grays to make their move. They just didn't have enough information to know what they'd do or who they'd target. There were too many variables.

"Guess I'm going to need to reschedule our date," he said.

"When you do, try not to look as relieved as you do right now." Dax raised a hand. "I know why. But take it from someone who has made that mistake already. It's okay to be pleased they'll be safe somewhere far from ground zero. It is not wise to let them *see* how happy you are about it."

"Noted. Any other words of wisdom before I go?"

"If you decide not to take the medi-bot treatment, that's fine. But make sure you're doing it for the right reasons. You're not your grandfather or your old man. You're my best friend, and I'd really like it if you were around for the next few centuries."

Dax's words hit hard. "Centuries? You're going to do it?" He hadn't expected anyone to make the decision so soon. But the thought of losing out on all that time with his friends... that was something he hadn't considered.

"Yeah. We decided last night."

"When are you doing it?"

"Not until the rest of the team has had more time to decide. We're not telling them yet."

"Just me?"

"Well, yeah." Dax smirked. "If I'm going to be signing on for an extended contract with this outfit, I want you to suffer along with me."

"I'll think about it." Kurt rose and nodded to Dax. "But not until tomorrow. Tonight we're all going to be busy."

"Stay sharp out there. And if you need backup, we're thirty seconds away." He laughed. "Well, most of us are. Nyx can get to you inside of ten seconds. Five if we let her break down a few walls along the way."

"Let's hope we don't need her to do that."

"Let's hope," Dax agreed.

They parted ways and Kurt was back in the main office two minutes later. The atmosphere wasn't so tense now, the energy close to normal instead of crackling like a reactor about to blow.

He dropped into his chair and pulled out his comm unit. There was nothing wrong with him sending her a note to make sure she was okay after being attacked.

Bobbi,

I'm sorry to hear you're not going to be there tonight. I was looking forward to our ice cream defensive. If you're interested, we could go for frozen desserts some other time, no dress uniform needed.

Hope your arm is healing well.
K.

He sent it before he changed his mind and then got back to work. It was going to be a long night, but with Bobbi safely out of the way, he had one less thing to worry about. The rest was up to his team, the station's corporate security, and the Gray Men. His gut told him that whatever they were planning, they'd make their move soon.

7

Kurt had thought last night's event was as dull and dry as it could get. He'd been wrong. The only thing worse than being at a formal party full of self-important guests was being at the same party twice. Oh, there were a few new faces in the crowd and different appetizers on the trays, but the whole affair was one déjà-vu moment after another. *Veth*, they were even telling the same tired jokes. Worse, they were laughing as if they'd never heard them before.

The only thing that made it bearable was the food. He tried whatever was on offer as various trays were carried by. Some of it was like the caviar, too strange to be truly tasty, but it was a way of passing the time, and everything he sampled was the real thing. Even the meat had been butchered from a living animal instead of grown in a vat.

The rest of the time he observed the guests and chatted with Colonel Scott's date for the evening. He had to look twice before he recognized the elegantly dressed woman as Phylomenia Harrington. She was a quick-witted, no-nonsense pilot who seemed to know everyone on the station by name and was somewhat of a den mother to the group of cyborgs over at the Nova Club.

They'd spent most of the time commenting on the attire of their fellow invitees and discussing the décor. The entire color scheme had been redone overnight. The carpet was a dark blue now, and the walls were white with silver and blue accents. He had no idea how Tianna had managed it, but apparently even magic was possible if you had enough money.

The staff were already bustling around the dining stations, even though dinner wouldn't be served for another hour. After that would be the speeches, with Tianna and Colonel Archer making announcements. From where he stood he could see the finishing touches being added to the dessert table, and it reminded him of Bobbi. She hadn't replied to his note and he was trying not to let that bother him, but he was glad she wasn't here tonight. She was safer at home.

Security all over the station had been ramped up in preparation for possible trouble from either the Grays or the civilians living here. Yesterday's protest had been relatively peaceful, but it wouldn't take much for things to turn ugly.

An uneasy tension lingered over the party, too. Factions were sticking closer together tonight, circling each other like fighters not quite ready to throw the first punch. The meetings had ended only an hour before the party, which meant he had no idea what had been decided, but judging by what he was seeing, negotiations hadn't gone well. *Typical*. He'd seen enough of these idiots to know that some of them would happily go to war with each other if it meant holding onto their profit margins.

Trinity's voice interrupted his musings. "Sabre. Check your six o'clock. You have incoming."

Kurt spun around to look, prepared to face whatever threat was coming his way... and found himself staring as the most beautiful woman he'd ever seen walked into view, making straight for him.

Bobbi. And by all the stars that shine, she looked good.

She'd traded her dress uniform for a curve-hugging, sleeveless, red velvet cocktail dress with a plunging V-neck that revealed a blood-heating amount of golden skin. Her dark hair, normally braided neatly, spilled over her shoulders in gleaming waves. She looked so good he momentarily forgot that she wasn't supposed to be here at all.

"Son of a starbeast. I knew she gave in too easily," Archer swore as he spotted his niece.

"You didn't know she was coming, sir?" Kurt asked.

"I did not," Archer said flatly.

Bobbi moved through the crowd with the grace of a dancer, drawing the eyes of every male present as she moved past. Kurt had a sudden urge to take off his jacket and wrap it around her very bare shoulders.

"Did you just growl?" Trinity asked in his ear.

"No," he muttered.

Trin snickered. "Must be a faulty mic."

He wasn't having this conversation right now. He needed to say something far more important, and it wasn't to Trinity.

Bobbi was still a few meters away when he walked over to meet her, deliberately putting himself between her and the colonel.

"You look amazing. I take it this is why you didn't answer my message about a rain check on the ice cream?"

She turned up the wattage on her smile until it nearly dazzled him. "I had no intention of missing our rendezvous. I just wanted it to be a surprise." She raised her hands and flung them outward. "Tada. Surprise."

"Oh, I'm surprised." He was also equal parts worried and delighted to see her. Her arrival meant he wouldn't be bored tonight. Not when he was going to have to spend time keeping her safe from any threat, including the half-dozen men loitering nearby, waiting for a chance to talk to her. That was *not* happening. Not on his watch.

He leaned in to murmur his next words into her ear. "I am also impressed. You clean up very nicely, Lieutenant Commander Castille."

"Thank you. For tonight, I'm just Bobbi." Her eyes narrowed slightly as she glanced over his shoulder, presumably at Archer. "As per the colonel's orders, Lieutenant Commander Castille is not attending this soirée."

"Do you think he's going to see it that way?"

Her eyes flashed and her lips thinned into a determined line. "He took me off his guest list. He never said I couldn't attend at someone else's invitation."

A light came on in the back of his lust-muddled brain. "Tianna?"

She flashed him a wicked little smile that sent half the blood in his body rushing south. This was a new side to her personality, and he liked it. Sass suited her. "Tianna," she confirmed. "Sometimes, it's good to have friends in high places."

"Lieutenant Commander Castille, if I could have a word?" Archer's voice was as cold as the void outside.

"Of course, Colonel Archer." She lifted her chin, winked at Kurt, and then stepped past him to speak with Archer.

Kurt stayed nearby, using the distraction of Bobbi's arrival to scan the crowd while everyone was looking elsewhere. Apart from the staff, who were all focused on their tasks, almost everyone else was watching Bobbi and Archer. No doubt they were hoping for more of last night's drama. He wanted to know who *wasn't* watching. Halverson looked on with an expression of carefully crafted outrage as fake as his hair color, but his ever-present aide was not at his side. "Find Clooney for me." He subvocalized.

"On it," Trinity replied.

He spotted Garrett Michaels leaning against a wall near the main doors. He looked relaxed and indifferent, but as their eyes met, the other man nodded, his lips quirking up into a ghost of a smile.

So, he wasn't the only one keeping an eye on things tonight. But who was he watching out for and why?

"Is someone watching Michaels?"

"Nyx is. Problem?"

"Not so far, but he's not here for the food."

Trinity swore under her breath. "Good thing we expanded the team or we wouldn't have enough bodies to track everyone."

"The way things are going, all the Nova Force teams will need more members."

"Or more teams. Then again, if Tianna can forge some kind of corporate alliance, maybe things will settle down again."

He chuckled but didn't answer. They both knew that whatever happened here, the corporations would never stop pushing the boundaries of what was legal in their quest for profit.

Trinity was quiet long enough for him to finish his scan of the crowd. He didn't see anything suspect, but he couldn't see the whole room.

Just as he relaxed, Trinity spoke again. "You won't be able to see him from your position, but there's another player on the board. Verner Lange just arrived, and he wasn't on the guest list Astek sent over this afternoon."

"Gate crasher?" he asked. Lange was a senior analyst for Nova Force. He had the means to be their spy, but so far they hadn't found any motivation. He was estranged from his family, had no real friends, and kept to himself most of the time. For him to attend a party of this caliber was out of character, which made him worth watching.

"Doesn't look like it. He's just a late addition. When

I get more information, I'll let you know. Aria is going to keep an eye on him."

He turned to check on Archer and Bobbi. The two seem to have settled their differences and were engaged in quiet conversation, but they were at an angle to him so he couldn't get a sense of what was being said.

He was about to do a circuit of the room and see if he could find Lange or Clooney when music started to play. It was a breezy, instrumental number just loud enough to drown out the conversations going on all around him. The crowd parted, giving way to a raised platform that slowly slid out from one of the walls. It took him a few seconds to recognize what it was—a dancefloor. Once it stopped moving, slots along the edges opened and a railing system rose into place to keep the dancers from stepping off the edge. The surface was dark blue with swirls of silver that pulsed and shifted in time to the music.

Bobbi reappeared at his side. He glanced down and then snapped his gaze higher. He absolutely was not going to stare down her dress like a teenage boy. *Nope.*

"You alright? You're looking a little pained," she asked.

"I'm fine. It's just that dress is…" he scrambled for a word that wouldn't leave him sucking on shoe leather for the rest of the night. Revealing? Risqué? He settled on "Wow."

"Wow, good?"

"Wow, *very* good." And now he was down to monosyllabic words. What about Bobbi reduced him to this state? Whatever it was, he needed it to stop. There was too much at stake for his brain's higher functions to go on hiatus whenever he got close to her.

"Thank you." She looked around the room and then at the raised dancefloor. To his surprise, she took his hand. "Dance with me?"

He should have said no. He was on duty. He needed to stay focused. But then he considered the raised platform and changed his mind. He'd be able to see the whole room from up there, and he'd get to do it while spending time with Bobbi. "It would be my pleasure."

He curled his fingers around hers and let her lead him up the stairs and onto the floor. She turned to face him and he drew her into his arms, one hand on her back, the other still clasped in hers.

As he guided her through the first few steps, she laughed. "And you were worried when I mentioned dancing the other day."

He bowed his head and drew her in until their bodies were almost touching, her mouth so close it would be easy to steal a kiss. *Veth*, he was tempted to do it, to give in to the need to know what she tasted like, how her body would feel pressed against his.

She looked up at him, lips parted, eyes wide, and he knew she was feeling the same pull he was.

He forced himself to raise his head and then made a confession to break the tension building between them. "After your warning, I might have spent a little time in the sim-pods practicing,"

"You did? Why?"

He wanted nothing more than to tell her everything. Why she was under investigation. How much he wanted her. The danger she was in just being here tonight. The fact he wanted to whisk her away somewhere quiet and kiss her until neither of them could think.

He managed to throttle back on that impulse and gave her a tiny portion of the truth instead. "Because I wanted to be prepared. Just in case I got a chance to ask a beautiful JAG officer if she would dance with me." He grinned. "Only as it turned out, she asked me first."

They moved around the floor, his attention split between the woman in his arms and the guests who filled the hall. His instincts were telling him he was missing something, but he couldn't see anything amiss.

Bobbi laughed. "It's my turn to be impressed. You're a good dancer, especially since you haven't stopped scanning the room since we started."

"Sorry." And he was. He would far prefer to be giving all his attention to her. She might be a suspect, and bad for his control, but he still couldn't stay away from her.

"Don't be. You're working. Most of these people have no idea the potential danger they're in." She moved her hand from his waist to place it on his chest. "I *do* know."

He slowed their dance, pulling her in hard against him before he could stop himself. "Then why are you here?"

"Because I need to be."

"Why? What are you up to?" he demanded, his voice hushed.

The song ended, but he didn't let her go. The next

tune was a slow waltz, and before he knew what she was doing Bobbi had her arms around his neck, her fingers brushing the back of his neck as she swayed to the music, still caught firmly in his arms.

"The same thing you are. I'm not allowed…" she frowned, clearly frustrated. "You're going to have to trust me. But there's something you need to know. I talked to Tiana's AI last night, and she did some checking for me. Halverson's invitation came directly from Astek Corp, but Tink can't figure out who sent it. It's like the system generated it all by itself."

There were plenty of ways that might have happened, but one possibility stood out from the rest. Someone, or something, had breached Astek Corp's computer network. It had happened before. The entire station had been infiltrated to various degrees. Not even the IAF's system was spared, though that incursion was limited to a security program not connected to the main network.

Eric, the team's cyber-security expert and computer wizard, had spent months chasing down leads that vanished before he could pin them down. He was convinced it was V.I.D.A, the sentient AI that Dr. Absalom, the Gray Men's chief scientist, had created and then unleashed on the galaxy. If the rogue program had managed to breach Astek Corporation's main system, it could do a lot more than just send out an invitation. It could control the doors, the robots, and even the environmental systems.

"Why didn't you tell anyone?" he demanded.

"Because Tink only sent me the information a little

while ago, and I'm under orders not to discuss things with your team until later. I've already told Tianna she needs to do a full check of all systems."

"Who ordered you not to tell me—uh—us about this?"

She shook her head. "I've already said too much. But you needed to know."

He hissed out a frustrated breath. "You need to get out of here. Now."

"No. I need to stay."

He wanted to shake her. Or kiss her. Or both. Instead, he let her go and stepped back, turning a full circle to look for Halverson. "Did you catch that, Trin?" he subvocalized.

"I did. Halverson is with Archer. If V.I.D.A or the Grays wanted the general here, nothing good can come of it," Trinity said.

"Agreed."

He looked down at Bobbi. "Who else knows?"

"Colonel Archer. I told him a few minutes ago."

"Let me guess. He took your warning *under advisement*?"

"Exactly. So, I'm telling you because I'm hoping you and your team will have more luck convincing him he needs to take this seriously."

"I'll see what I can do. But you need to leave. Promise me you'll find somewhere else to be for the rest of the night."

She looked around the room one last time, as if drinking it all in, and then sighed. "Okay. But now you really do owe me an ice cream date."

They made their way back to the stairs and down to the main floor. Instead of descending the last step with him, she stopped, taking advantage of the extra height to kiss him lightly on the cheek. "Be careful."

Fraxx it. He turned his head and captured her lips with his. A sun bloomed in his chest, fire streaking through his veins as he finally took what he'd been dreaming about for too many nights.

She leaned into the kiss with an almost silent moan he felt more than heard, and for one perfect moment, time slowed. Just the two of them existed alone—no dangers and no distractions.

It couldn't have been more than a few seconds, but when he lifted his head again, the world had changed. Everything seemed brighter, colors more vivid, and the taste of her lips was forever branded on his senses.

"Later, we're going to do more of that. Also, ice cream. And talk. But for now, you have to go. I need to know you're safe."

"We really need to work on our timing. Stay in one piece, please." And with that, she was gone. He tracked down Archer and was waiting for a chance to catch him alone when something made him turn to check on Bobbi one last time.

Son of a bitch. She hadn't left. In fact, she was on the far side of the room from the door. What was she up to?

He had a choice to make. If Bobbi had lied to him about Halverson's invitation, she'd done it without a single tell. He believed her. But why tell him now? Was it really a warning or just a way to distract him? Did he talk to Archer or follow Bobbi?

It didn't take him long to make a decision. Archer could take care of himself. He needed to know what Bobbi was doing. "Trin. Castille didn't leave the party. I need to follow her. Can you send someone else to cover Archer?"

"Sending in Chaos. If there's trouble, Nyx can protect him better than anyone else."

"Agreed."

"Your non-compliant JAG officer is either really clumsy, or she just pulled a bump and switch with Clooney. Now he's headed for a side door and she's wandered off to... no. Correction. She's now following Clooney. It's a staff only door fifteen meters ahead of you. Windowed. Clearly marked. You can't miss it."

"Thank you."

"Fido says you are to track down your girlfriend and find out what's going on. Magi says welcome to the club."

He bulldozed his way through the crowd who quickly got the hint and cleared a path for him. "I know I'm going to regret this, but what club?"

Trin laughed. "Apparently it's the guys who like dangerous women club."

"Bobbi is not dangerous. She's just stubborn and has issues with authority." *And might have just done some kind of exchange with a potential member of the Gray Men...*

"Uh huh. What happened to your concern she might be a spy?"

"I don't kiss spies. Therefore, she can't be one. This conversation is over."

A server carrying a tray of drinks came through the

door, giving him a view of the corridor beyond. Bobbi was near the end of the hall, shoes in hand as she turned and vanished around a corner.

He ducked through the door and followed as quickly as he could. She wasn't getting away from him, and when he caught up to her this time, he was going to get some answers.

8

WHEN WERE the men in her life going to stop trying to keep her safe? First her uncle and then Kurt. It was ridiculous. She was a grown woman. An IAF officer for *fraxx* sake. And Scott had been the one to bring her into this investigation.

Bobbi had no intentions of leaving the party, no matter what Lieutenant Commander Pain in the Ass said, even if she did want to climb him like a jungle gym. When she'd kissed his cheek, she had no idea how he'd react. They were in public, with his team no doubt watching on surveillance, but after their dance, she hadn't been able to resist the chance to touch him again. She'd never expected him to turn and kiss her back. *Re'veth*, it had been a hell of a kiss, too. She definitely wanted more of that please. And soon.

She was still caught up in her conflicted feelings about Kurt when she spotted a familiar face—one that had no reason to be at the party. Verner Lange was a recluse by nature, so what was he doing here? He was one of the names on her list of suspects, but as of this morning, he hadn't been on the guest list. Yet here he was, hovering near a table set out with pitchers of water and juice for those guests who deigned to pour their own drinks.

She altered course, making her way slowly to the table as if she had all the time in the world and nothing on her mind but a need for a cold drink. She was still some distance away when a second suspect arrived at the table. Lieutenant Clooney wandered up with deliberate casualness, and Bobbi's instincts screamed that something was about to happen. She managed to keep an eye on the two men as she walked, slowing her steps so she didn't disrupt things.

Even though she was watching for *something* to happen, when the handoff came it was so quick she almost missed it. Lange set a palm-sized, silver container down on the table, partially hiding it behind a pitcher of jazza berry juice. He poured himself a glass of water and walked away, leaving the container behind. A second later, Clooney picked up the object, slid it up his sleeve and then served himself a glass of juice without missing a beat.

The whole thing had taken seconds, and both men acted with a level of professionalism that didn't fit with their normal personas. She needed to inform the colonel, but to send him a message she'd have to take her eyes off Clooney. She had the feeling if she did that she'd lose him and any chance of finding out what was going on.

This was why she'd pushed her uncle so hard about

sharing information with Kurt's team. Not just so they had all the intel, but because they were the one thing she was missing—backup.

Since she didn't have anyone to call on, she would have to do this the hard way. Alone. Again. She set off for the table at an unsteady pace, a too-wide smile plastered on her face. As she walked, she slipped a hand into her pocket and pulled out a micro-tracker. When the colonel had offered her off-the-record access to the quartermaster's stores, he'd done it so she would have everything she needed to work on his secret project. She'd taken the opportunity to pick up a couple of other, more interesting items, including a few trackers and a wafer-thin comm device that was tucked into the same discreet pocket of her dress.

Clooney moved away from the table before she got there, but by some fluke he chose a path that intersected with hers. She stumbled into him and managed to transfer the tracker to the back of his uniform.

"Sorry, Lieutenant. One too many of those tasty cocktails on an empty stomach."

"Yes. Indeed." He looked down his nose at her. "I was under the impression you were not attending tonight."

She waved a hand vaguely. "Colonel uninvited me, someone else re-invited me. I have friends in high places. Now, I'm off to find some water and clear my head. Sorry again."

She tottered off and made herself count to three before she turned back to look. Clooney was walking away from her, so she turned and followed him, keeping a discreet distance.

She needn't have bothered. He never looked back. He walked through the crowd and straight through a door marked Staff Only, vanishing from sight. She did the only thing she could think of and followed him.

On the far side of the door was a different world. Luxury gave way to practicality. Soft lights and deep colors were replaced with bright lights, beige walls, and scuffed tile floors.

The heels would make too much noise on the tiles so she stopped just long enough to take them off. She couldn't do anything about her red dress, which stood out like a signal flare. She'd just have to go slowly and make sure he didn't spot her.

It wasn't hard to figure out which way he'd gone. When she reached the end of the corridor there was only one way to turn, so she peered carefully around the corner hoping to see where he'd gone. All she saw was a short hallway that led to a door marked Exit.

Fraxx. She hurried to the door and opened it, checking left and then right for any sign of her quarry. The halls beyond were empty. She had a moment of panic before she remembered the tracker.

"I'm an idiot," she muttered and pulled the almost flat comm device from her pocket. It had minimal functionality, but she'd loaded it with a program that was linked to the trackers she'd purloined.

Her hands were shaking as she activated the device and the software. "Got you," she declared in a triumphant whisper and set off after her target.

After a few minutes, his destination was obvious. He was heading for the private docking rings that had been set aside strictly for the use of Astek's illustrious guests.

He'd reach the ships soon. Too soon for anyone to stop him. Even if she told someone where to find him, he'd likely be gone before the IAF or Corp-Sec could reach them, not with security stretched so thin because of the unrest and protests... which she now suspected were part of the plan all along. The IAF's ships were all docked on the far side of the station, and no one wanted to start a firefight with Astek Station in the middle.

Bobbi's mind raced as she followed Clooney, her bare feet making no noise on the cold metal floor. Between Kurt's kiss and the excitement of the chase, she could be walking on ice right now and still wouldn't notice the chill.

The docking rings were quiet save for a handful of bots scuttling back and forth. She fell in behind one that was pulling a trolley full of food dispenser packets. It wasn't perfect cover, but if Clooney turned, she should have time to duck out of sight. At least, that was the theory. If she was lucky, she wouldn't have to test it.

She had a plan now. And a ship—if she could get to it. Her uncle couldn't dock his personal vessel with the IAF's fleet without raising a few eyebrows, but he'd wanted it somewhere secure. Tianna had offered him a berth with the other guests' ships, which meant it was on this side of the station. Scott had given her the berth number and access codes in case of emergency, and this was definitely one.

Whatever Clooney was up to, she knew better than to try and take him down with nothing but a shoe, her new medi-bots and some mostly forgotten combat classes. There'd be weapons aboard the *Bat*, though. If she could follow him, maybe she could find out more about what the Grays were up to.

It was a dangerous, stupid plan and she knew it. It was also the only plan she had.

She breathed a sigh of relief when he walked past the section where the *Bat* was docked. She ducked down a short corridor and found the right berth. Her hands were shaking so hard she messed up the access code the first time, but she got it right on the second try.

The door slid open and she started to step inside. Then, a hard hand gripped her shoulder and spun her around. She squeaked in undignified surprise as her attacker pushed her up against the side of the *Bat* and growled. It was Kurt, and he looked mad enough to chew through hull plating.

"When I told you to leave the party, this was not what I had in mind. What the *fraxx* are you up to, Bobbi? And whose ship is this?"

She pressed a finger to her lips. "Keep your voice down. Do you want him to hear us?"

Kurt's scowl deepened. "You mean Clooney? We saw your little bump and switch earlier. What did he give you? How long have you been working with him?"

Shock and anger swirled in her gut. He thought she was with Clooney? Still? If he thought that, why the hell had he kissed her? "What? No! You've got it all wrong. Come in. I'll explain."

"Damn right you're going to explain."

He stepped away from her. The moment there was space enough to move, she turned and dashed inside. Her heart was slamming against her ribs and enough adrenaline cruised through her system to keep her awake for a week, but she had to stay calm. If Clooney got too far away, the tracker's signal would fade and they'd lose him.

"Boo, are you online?"

"Affirmative. Hello, Roberta," the ship's AI greeted her in a masculine voice that was remarkably like her uncle's.

Kurt stomped in behind her. "What the hell is a Boo? Whose ship is this?"

She ignored him for the moment. "Boo, prep for emergency departure. If I give you tracking data from a comm unit, can you transfer it to your systems?"

"Of course."

"Dammit, Bobbi! Stop. You're not going anywhere until I know what's happening."

She turned to show him the tracking app on her comms, but the words froze in her throat. Kurt had drawn his sidearm and was aiming it at her.

"You're going to shoot me?" she asked softly, her heart battered by so many conflicting emotions she couldn't have named them all.

For a terrible moment, silence loomed. Then he shook his head. The gun vanished into whatever concealed holster he wore, and she found she could breathe again.

"So, we're back to you trusting me again? How many times are we going to go through this? Because honestly, I'm not sure my heart can take much more."

His hazel eyes darkened. "There's an easy way to fix this. Tell me what's going on."

"Okay." She organized her thoughts quickly. She had one shot at this. Time to make the best presentation of her life, and she was the one on trial.

Somedays the universe was a nice, logical place where things made sense. Today was not one of those days. Hell, it hadn't been one of those months. But nothing he'd been through had prepared him for this. He was holding a gun on the woman he wanted more than his next breath, hoping like hell she wasn't the spy he was hunting.

When she asked if he was going to shoot her, Kurt had heard so much more than her words. Pain lurked there as well as confusion and fear. *Fraxx*, she was afraid of him.

He put away the gun. Whatever happened next, he knew in his heart he wouldn't need it.

"So, we're back to you trusting me again? How many times are we going to go through this? Because honestly, I'm not sure my heart can take much more."

He didn't know how many more times his heart could take this either. He wanted to go to her, shake her, and then wrap her in his arms and hold her until the hurt in her eyes faded away. He didn't. He couldn't. Not yet. "There's an easy way to fix this. Tell me what's going on."

"Okay." And then she told him the truth. She was poised, eloquent, and to the point. By the time she was done, he'd fallen just a little bit more in love with her. She told him she'd been brought in to double check Nova Force's work, but once she saw the handoff, she'd decided to follow Clooney on her own. The thought made him want to turn her over his knee and spank her ass pink. Her investigatory skills were damned good, but the risk she'd taken… *Veth*.

Still, she'd told him enough. Not all of it. Not even close, but enough for him to know two things. He believed her. And that meant he needed to follow Clooney.

"Alright."

Her eyes widened just a little. "That's all I get? Really? Because I think that story is worth at least a *fraxx* or two."

"I'll swear at you later. Busy now. Trinity, I need Rossi's authorization to commandeer this vessel and go after our suspect."

"You have it," Dax said, surprising him. "Trinity is arranging for Halverson to be taken in for questioning regarding his aide's actions. Archer is staying put. Nyx is on her way to the *Malora* to get her engines warmed up. We'll catch up to you. Go."

"Gone, sir."

He held out his hand to Bobbi. "I need you to give

me that comm unit so I can track Clooney. Then, you are disembarking." He pointed to the door.

"The hell I will. You'd still be at the party looking for spies if it weren't for me. I'm not leaving." She flashed him a wicked smile that worried and aroused him at the same time. "Besides, Boo isn't going to listen to you. You don't have authorization."

"Then get me authorized," he said through gritted teeth. There was no way in hell she was coming on this mission.

"And if I say no?"

"Then I'll get it from the owner. Who is it?" Private vessels were insanely expensive. This one had to belong to one of Astek's guests. It wasn't new, but it was luxurious. Deep blue furnishings, soft cream walls, partial bulkheads that broke the space into several sections, including what looked like a dining area with a real wood table. Who the hell owned it, and why did Bobbi have the access codes?

Her smile grew brighter and some instinct warned him he really wasn't going to like her answer.

"Colonel Scott Archer. I imagine he's a little busy right now, though. You may have to wait."

His control shattered. "Why the hell do you have access to Archer's private ship? Is he an ex-lover? Maybe a current one?"

A look of horror wiped the smile off Bobbi's face. "Lover? Scott? Holy *fraxx*, no. Also yuck. He is not my type. He's my uncle! A fact I have gone to great lengths to hide since I joined up since it would complicate my career no end."

Kurt blinked. His mouth opened and closed several times, but no words came out. "Uncle?"

"Uncle Scott. Yes. My mothers gave him this ship and I've flown on it several times. He made sure I knew where it was berthed in case of emergency." She stormed over and poked him in the chest. "Did you really think I'd kiss you if I were involved with someone else?"

"It crossed my mind."

She rolled her eyes. "For a brilliant investigator, you can be a surprisingly bad judge of character."

"And for a JAG officer with no combat experience, you take a lot of risks," he shot back.

"I get that from the Archer side of the family. Or so my mothers tell me. Now, we can discuss this further, or we can go after the bad guy. Which one is it going to be?"

She was right. They didn't have time for this. "Alright. You can stay on board. But you will do what I say. You will not take any more unnecessary risks. And once we're on our way, I want a full account of all the things you didn't mention in your summary of events."

"Boo. Add Lieutenant Commander Kurt Bossyboots as an official guest."

"Done. Welcome aboard, Lieutenant Commander."

"Did you just tell the computer my name was Bossyboots?"

She arched a brow, and for one rather disturbing moment she reminded him of her uncle. "If the boot fits…"

"I like her. Can we keep her?" Trinity chimed in over his earpiece.

"I second that motion," Aria said.

"Do you have me on broadcast mode, Trinity?"

"We're on our way to the *Malora*. Group channel while we move. Didn't Fido tell you?"

"No. He did not." And when he saw his commander again, he was going to figure out a way to kick his ass for that little oversight.

While he was talking, Bobbi moved further into the ship, toward what he assumed was the flight deck. He turned and followed her, removing the throat mic and earpiece as he went. If they needed him, they could contact him through standard comms. He'd have to establish ship-to-ship communication once they were moving anyway.

Bobbi set a small comm unit on a scanner. "Ready, Boo. Scan and lock onto the signal. Where it goes, we go. Do you understand. I need you to be ready to follow that signal, even if the ship carrying it activates its jump drives."

"Understood. Do you wish me to inform you when it moves again?"

"I do."

"And do you wish for me to act as pilot?" the AI asked.

"Yes," Bobbi said.

"No," he interjected. "Boo, you're navigating. I'll be piloting."

"What? Why? Boo can handle it. Plus, this ship has stealth capability."

"No, Boo cannot handle it. We'll have to follow Clooney without looking like that's what we're doing. AIs are wonderful tools, but they have limits. You told it to follow and that's exactly what it will do. With all the subtly of a sledgehammer." He shot her a frustrated look. "And if we activate stealth mode, we're invisible to everyone, which means we run a real risk of getting smacked into by one of the other ships out there."

Her lips thinned, but she didn't argue with him. "I hadn't thought of that."

"That's because you're not trained for this." He pointed to the copilot's chair, which looked like it had never been used. "Strap in."

He sat in the other chair and started familiarizing himself with the controls. He wasn't the best pilot on the team, but Dax made sure everyone had some experience flying the *Malora* and her shuttle. This wouldn't be much different.

"Boo. Get us clearance for takeoff but leave pilot control to me. Also, establish an encrypted comm link with the IAF Frigate *Malora*." He paused. "You can do that. Right?"

The AI managed to sound indignant. "Of course. Colonel Archer would never use an unencrypted channel."

"Of course he wouldn't," he muttered under his breath. "And who the hell names their AI Boo?"

"It's short for *Bat Out of Hell*, which is the name of the ship."

He stopped and turned to stare at Bobbi. He could not have heard her correctly. Archer didn't have a whimsical bone in his body. Did he? "Repeat that, please."

"The ship. It's the *Bat Out of Hell*. Uncle Scott named her himself." She shook her head. "I was lobbying for him to call her the Celestial Jewel."

"After your mothers, Juliana and Celeste?" The question made him pause. "So, which one of them is Archer's sister, and why isn't there any record of it?"

"Mama Celeste is his older sister. As for why there's no record? It's because she fell out with her parents and cut ties a long time ago. They had her whole life mapped out, and she wanted no part in their plans. She wanted to help people, not corporations. Ironically, my other mother became everything they wanted Celeste to be...and they've never met her. Or me. The rifts on that side are deep enough to fit a planet between them."

"But Archer crossed the rift?" It was hard to imagine the by-the-book man he knew taking time to reach out to a rebellious sister. Then again, it was hard to believe that same man would name his ship what he had. Apparently, he had hidden depths... and a really hot niece. *Veth*. His life was getting more complicated by the second.

Bobbi snorted with laughter. "You only know Colonel Archer. I didn't meet that version of my uncle until he brought me out here and got me to check into your team."

That still rankled. He understood the reasons, but he didn't like it. "So while we've been investigating you,

you've been investigating us, and all of us have been chasing the same leads trying to catch the spy?"

"It was not my idea. In fact, I've been trying to get him to agree to let me tell you everything." She paused. "Uh, I mean, tell your team everything."

"For a lawyer, you don't lie very well."

"One of my mothers would agree with you. The other would say that if I have to lie to win, the case was never worth winning."

The AI interrupted before he could reply. "Attention. The source of the signal I am tracking has moved. Do you wish me to display current location?"

"Yes," he and Bobbi said together.

A holo-map shimmered into existence over the console, showing Astek Station, their ship, and a small vessel highlighted in red. Their departure clearance had already come in, but he took a moment to calculate the route least likely to tip off Clooney he'd grown a tail.

"What are we waiting for?" Bobbi asked.

"If we take off now, he'll notice us. We'll wait a bit and then ease out so we blend in with the rest of the traffic."

She shot him a bemused look. "So, your whole plan is to fly casually?"

"You could say that."

She snickered. He had no idea why.

"I have an incoming message for you, Roberta," Boo said.

"From who?" she asked.

"Colonel Scott Archer."

Bobbi groaned. "Did you alert him to our presence here?"

"Of course. That is part of my programming."

"You deal with your uncle. I'm going to move us away from the station," Kurt said.

"Not being on screen won't save you, you know." Bobbi smirked and then faced straight ahead and accepted the incoming message. Archer's face appeared on the main monitor. "Hi, Uncle Scott."

"You're stealing my ship. And outing our relationship. The one you made me take such pains to hide."

"I'm borrowing it, yes. And uh... sorry. It was necessary. Kurt thought I was taking this ship without permission."

"You are."

"I'm not. You gave me the access codes yourself. Do you really want to argue the law with me? I'm a lawyer. Remember?"

"I do. Which makes me wonder what my niece, the JAG officer, is doing in the middle of an active Nova Force investigation I ordered her off of."

"I'm doing what you brought me out here to do. I'm hunting down the spy. Well, one of them."

Archer's expression turned to stone. "You're out of your depth, Bobbi. This is dangerous."

"I'll make sure nothing happens to her, sir," Kurt said, taking a moment to join the conversation.

"You'd better. If anything happens to her..." Archer left the rest of the threat unsaid.

"I know. You'll toss my ass out the nearest airlock, sir."

Archer snorted. "It's not me you need to worry about, Meyer. You should be afraid of her mothers. Take care of my niece and my ship, in that order. I need to go. Astor is about to make her speech, and then it's my turn. Keep communications to a minimum. No direct contact with me from now on. *Malora* only. The fewer people realize you're linked to the IAF, the better off you are. The *Bat* is combat capable, but she's no warship. Good luck. Good hunting."

"Thank you, sir," Kurt said.

"Be careful, sir. We know about two spies, now. There might be more."

Archer didn't answer, except to nod sharply. Then, the screen went blank.

"That went better than I expected," Bobbi said, sinking back into her seat.

Kurt grunted in acknowledgment, but he wasn't sure he agreed with her assessment. This morning he'd thought his life was complicated, and that was when he thought Bobbi was a possible spy. Now, that seemed like a simpler time. She wasn't a spy. She was Archer's *fraxxing* niece, and his partner for this mission. He was never taking Dax's advice on dating again.

Then, he looked over at Bobbi, and a little voice whispered that maybe he wouldn't need that kind of advice in the future. He'd just have to keep them both alive long enough to find out.

9

AFTER THE EXCITEMENT of discovering the spy and the adrenaline-fueled chase that followed, Bobbi was flying high. She wanted to be doing something. Anything. But instead she was sitting in the copilot's chair, reduced to watching a screen as Kurt flew painfully slowly after their quarry.

They were clear of the station now, but so far Clooney hadn't activated his jump drive. She sat on the edge of her seat and waited. Surely he wasn't going to obey the rules of navigation and stick to standard engines for the next few hours? If he did that, they'd never be able to follow him.

Kurt gave her an amused look. "You really want him to run so we can chase him. Don't you?"

"Don't you? The waiting is killing me."

"Waiting is a big part of the job. Once he jumps, Boo will calculate vectors and we'll go after him. After that, we'll be traveling for however long it takes. It could be days, or weeks, and we won't be able to confirm his destination until he drops back into normal space."

"And then we go after him?"

"Maybe. Depends where he goes. We may need to wait for the *Malora*."

"And I thought the wheels of justice moved slowly."

"It's all part of the same machine. Investigations take time too."

She wrinkled her nose. "It's just that after everything happening so fast, it's hard to slow down again."

"I know. But we have to." He pivoted in his chair so he was facing her. "Especially you. There's too much you don't know about this side of things. You're a lawyer, not law enforcement."

"I got us this far," she reminded him.

"You did. But you put yourself in danger doing it. You don't know anything about surveillance or avoiding notice. If Clooney had noticed you, what was your excuse for being away from the party? What would you have done if he'd attacked you, or worse, shot you outright?

"That didn't happen." She knew she'd been lucky, but she had also been careful.

"No. But it could have. Next time, it might. So, we are going to do this my way, and that means you do what I say, when I say it."

Her body and her head had very different reactions to his statement. Her head wanted to tell him to dive out the nearest airlock. Her body, however, was a traitorous bitch that found his dominance arousing. She wanted to unstrap herself and curl up in his lap so badly it was almost a physical ache. She could still taste his kisses, and the memory of being pressed up against his hard body had her fingers drifting down to the release button on her harness.

"And if I don't?"

"Then I will do whatever it takes to keep you safe. You heard your uncle. If I don't bring you back in one piece, they'll never find my body."

She waved a hand. "He's exaggerating."

"Maybe. Even so, if you get hurt, my career options go up in smoke."

She couldn't argue with him there. Scott had made it clear he was responsible for her safety. "Okay. I'm willing to agree to do what you say, but only when we're in a dangerous situation."

He opened his mouth to argue, but before he could say anything, the view on the monitor changed. Clooney's ship was gone.

"The target has activated their jump drive. I am calculating the most likely— calculations complete," Boo announced, interrupting itself.

Kurt's hands flew over the console, leaving her to watch in silent admiration. Within seconds, the jump engines came online. The transition was so smooth she barely felt it.

Kurt opened a comms channel. "*Malora*, you locked on?"

This time Dante replied. "We are. Transitioning in two minutes."

"Copy."

Kurt closed the channel and shifted his focus to the monitor ahead of him, his fingers tapping and twisting as he scrolled through screens of data. Finally, he exhaled and leaned back in his chair. "I hope your uncle keeps this ship well-stocked. It looks like we'll be in transit for a minimum of three days. It should be more, but Clooney's ship is faster than I expected. Good thing this one is too. We'll be able to keep up, barely. But the *Malora* won't. They're going to fall behind over time."

"How far behind?"

He spun his chair around to face her. "Depends entirely on where Clooney is headed and how hard our pilot pushes the engines. Could be a few hours, or it might be days."

"Days? We might have to wait for days for backup? That's insane."

"No, going into a dangerous situation without backup and limited resources is insane. It's also a good way to get dead. Dead people do not make good investigators. And I've heard it's a real bitch to arrest someone from the afterlife."

She huffed out a breath that was part frustration and part laughter. "Good point. Oh, and about the food situation, Scott likes his comforts, so I'm sure he keeps the food dispensers well-stocked. He's been working here a lot lately. He thought it was more secure than his office."

"He was probably right about that."

They both lapsed into thoughtful silence as the weight of the truth settled into their awareness. Spies. Hacks. Security breaches. None of it was theoretical anymore. The Gray Men were a threat the likes of which humanity, and possibly this entire part of the galaxy, had never seen before. If they weren't defeated, everything she believed in would be threatened. There would be no justice. No equality. No freedom.

"We can't let them win." She hadn't meant to speak the words aloud, but there they were, hanging in the air between them.

"We won't." Then he frowned. "I mean, me and my team won't. You've done your part."

She looked around at the empty ship. "Your team isn't here. I am."

"My team is close by, and they're trained for this." He unclipped himself from his harness and leaned toward her, making the cockpit suddenly feel far smaller. "You, on the other hand were ready to take this ship and fly off solo. No plan. No backup. I've seen your files, Bobbi. You were never regular military. You have no combat training or experience. You've got basic firearms certification, and that's it."

"But I'm here." She met his gaze and felt an instant rush of desire. She did her best to ignore it, but even as she argued with him, it was impossible to forget that they were finally alone together… on a ship with one bed.

"And here is where you're going to stay. On this ship. Out of danger."

"I'm an officer in the Intergalactic Armed Forces, not a delicate flower you need to protect."

"You already agreed to do as I say." He rose to his feet and then stared down at her from his full height.

She undid her harness and got to her feet. In bare feet she barely reached his shoulder, but she stood toe-to-toe with him and refused to back down. "I agreed to listen to you when we're in a dangerous situation."

She folded her arms over her chest, both to enforce her words and to reduce the temptation to do something foolish, like reach for him. "We're perfectly safe at the moment."

"You think we're safe? We're on a ship with limited weapons and shielding, chasing after someone who is in league with the most dangerous cabal in the galaxy. We have no idea what his ship's abilities are or what kind of man he really is because nothing in either of our investigations indicated he was capable of this kind of action. He's supposed to be a mediocre officer who only got promoted because his parents donated a stupid amount of scrip to the right causes. By all accounts he's nothing more than a manipulative sleaze riding his way up through the ranks on Halverson's coattails." He jabbed a finger at the screen. "Clearly, he's a lot more than that. Which means we missed it. If we missed him, we could have missed other things."

Kurt's jaw clenched, and he spoke his next words through closed teeth. "From here on in, there's no such thing as safe. Just varying degrees of danger."

"That's a little dramatic. Isn't it?"

"No, it's not. Tell me. What was your plan, exactly? Assuming you managed to follow him to his destination without him noticing you, what next?"

"I was going to tell Scott where I was and what I

was doing. I assumed he'd send you and your team after me."

"Uh huh. And would you have waited for us?"

She could tell by the way his mouth quirked up at one corner that he knew what her answer would be already. "No. I'd have followed him."

"And confronted him?"

"Maybe." She really hadn't thought that far ahead. It galled her that he was right, but that didn't change the fact he had a point. Several, in fact.

"So, your plan, such as it was, was to steal a ship you aren't qualified to pilot, to chase after a dangerous suspect to an unknown location. Once there, you were going to try to apprehend him alone. What were you going to do, exactly? Argue with him until he surrendered? You're not even armed!"

"I don't know! I hadn't thought about it. I was reacting, not planning. I know that's not smart, but it's all I could do."

"It wasn't. You could have told me what you'd done. Or Archer. Anyone. But you went off alone." His hands cupped her shoulders. "You could have died tonight."

"But I didn't."

"Thank the stars for that."

His eyes darkened, and she felt the pull between them intensify until it was almost too strong to resist. Just as she considered giving in, he spoke again. "You will not risk yourself like that again."

"That's my choice to make, not yours."

His hands tightened on her shoulders and his next

words came out with a hint of a snarl. "Dammit, Bobbi. Don't push me on this. You've got to listen."

"I'll listen when you stop treating me like a Tiskalian ice orchid. I'm tougher than that."

He growled in frustration. "I know you are, but if something happened to you…"

She threw out her next words like a challenge. "What? You're afraid it might wreck your career?"

He tangled one hand in her hair, cupped her cheek with the other, and then stared down at her with eyes aglow with desire. "No, little minx. I'm afraid it would break my heart."

He dropped his head and kissed her with a primal intensity that bordered on savage. His hand tightened in her hair as his mouth claimed hers.

All her anger and adrenaline were replaced by a firestorm of pure desire that burned away every thought save one. She wanted him, and there wasn't anything stopping her from acting on that need. Not anymore.

She reached up, took hold of his uniform near the collar, and used it to pull herself up as she kissed him back. His mouth raked across hers as he wrapped an arm like a steel bar across the small of her back and pulled her in tightly against him. It was like being pressed against a solid wall of heat and muscle.

She parted her lips on a low moan, and he swept his tongue into her mouth to tangle with hers. He released her hair, and a moment later his hands were on her hips. "Hold on to me."

Of all the orders he'd tried to give her lately, this

was one she was happy to obey. She wrapped her arms around his neck without breaking their kiss. He picked her up and carried her out of the cockpit. She thought he'd take her to one of the couches, but he took a few steps, pivoted, and then she found herself pressed up against a section of cold, hard bulkhead.

He kept their bodies welded together with one hard thigh pressing between her legs. She kept one arm around his neck and reached down to tug her dress up, freeing her legs so she could twine them around his waist. He groaned and rocked his hips against her, grinding his cock against her mound.

He kept her pinned to the wall with his weight and started a slow exploration of her body, working steadily upward until he found her breasts. Every touch made her nerves sing, and every kiss added fuel to the fire already burning in her blood. He toyed with her nipples through the gown, stroking and pinching until they were both diamond-hard nubs. Every touch sent a bolt of heat straight to her throbbing clit. Her senses reeled as she drank in every detail of this moment. Hard body. Heated touches. The hunger and need that tore through them both, the way he groaned her name.

He raised his head, eyes locked on hers. This close to him, she could see the starburst of golden brown within the green of his eyes. "Tell me you're okay with this." His voice was little more than a growl now, all gravel and need.

"Yes. I want this. Want you." She grinned up at him. "And we've got at least three days with nothing else to do. Right?"

His answering grin was as wicked as the devil himself. "Right."

Eventually, Kurt would need to think up a way to keep his stubborn little minx safe while he went after Clooney. Not to mention he still had to assess their situation, make plans, and coordinate with the rest of his team. But none of that was going to happen any time soon. Not when he finally had a chance to get tangled up and naked with Bobbi.

"Boo, take over all piloting and navigation duties. Engage privacy mode and do not interrupt unless our target changes flight patterns or we get a message from the *Malora*."

"Order confirmed," the AI replied, and once again Kurt was struck by how much it sounded like Archer. That was disturbing on a whole host of levels.

"Later, we're going to find out if there's a way to change that thing's voice patterns. It's like your uncle is here with us right now."

Bobbi burst into horrified giggles that were utterly adorable. "Ugh. Best we fix that."

"Uh-huh. But later."

"Much, much later."

As much as he hated to do it, Kurt moved away from the wall and then let her slip gently to the floor. "I like that dress too much to tear it off you, but if it's not gone in the next ten seconds, I make no promises as to its survival."

"Given it's the only item of clothing I own, please don't tear it." She touched the back of her neck and the dress unzipped itself. She let it slide down her body to pool at her feet, and for a moment, he forgot to breathe.

"You are stunning," he murmured a moment later. He was trying to stay in control, but it was a losing fight. She pushed all his buttons and refused to back down, even when it was the smart thing to do.

Bobbi smiled and then leaned over, her hair falling forward to hide her breasts as she stripped out of her red lace panties and let them fall to the floor atop her dress.

He stared and then swallowed hard. He could take this slowly. He had to.

His lovely minx straightened up, tossed back her hair, and smiled impishly. "Need some help figuring out the buttons?"

"You really don't want to tease me right now, minx. I'm a man on the edge."

She grinned. "I know. I want to find out what happens when I push you over it."

The last of his control shattered like ice dropped on marble.

"Wish granted." He grasped the collar of his shirt in both hands and pulled. Buttons flew off in all directions, but he had his shirt off in seconds, and that was all he cared about. He didn't bother stripping the rest of the way. He tore open his pants and left them slung around his hips as he pushed her up against the wall again, his mouth slanting across hers. *Veth*, he couldn't get enough of her. He craved the taste and scent of her, the feel of her skin beneath his hands, the sound of her breathy little moans as he touched her.

She writhed against him, the friction making his cock impossibly hard. She reached into his pants and wrapped her fingers around his length, drawing a low growl from deep within his chest.

She laid her free hand on his chest and then slid it higher, letting her nails glide along his skin with just enough force to sting a little. He closed his teeth on her lower lip, and she shivered in response, her nails pressing in a little deeper.

There were no sweet words or flowery promises. Tenderness would have to wait for another time. He fisted a hand in her hair, loving the warm weight of it wrapped around his fingers and the way she let him take control without backing down. He pulled her head to one side, baring her throat so he could drop several open-mouthed kisses down the side of her neck, biting her a little with each kiss.

She pumped his cock with firm, deliberate strokes that set his blood boiling and ramped up his need even more. He continued to kiss his way down her body to the swell of her soft breasts. She was a perfect handful, fitting into his palm as if she'd been made for him. He flicked a finger across one taut nipple, watching as she reacted with a needy moan, her back arching to offer herself up to him. He suckled each breast in turn and then rose up to kiss her again. He fucked her mouth with his tongue, matching the rhythm of her hand as she pumped his cock. He was close, but he didn't want to come until he was inside her, and he needed to do something first.

"Need to taste you."

"Is that what you need?" She ran a finger around the crown of his dick and then dragged it across the tip. "You sure?"

"You are hell bent on trying to break me. Aren't you?"

"Is it working?"

"*Fraxx*, yes."

"Good. I think we've both been holding back long enough. Don't you?"

He kissed the corner of her mouth and then dropped to his knees in front of her. "No more holding back. But remember, you wanted this."

He pushed her back against the wall and then wrapped a hand behind her knee and drew one leg over his shoulder. He turned his head, kissing the inside of her thigh, and then moved in close, her legs parting as he wedged himself between them and straightened until his mouth was level with her pussy. He cupped her ass with his free hand and drew her forward as he buried his head between her thighs.

She quivered and moaned as the taste of her filled his senses, learning what she liked and what she needed with every flick and lick of his tongue. True to his word, he wasn't gentle, nor did he play fair. Everything he learned, he used against her until she was rocking her hips against his mouth, her fingers buried in his hair as she reached for an orgasm he denied her time and again. She wanted him broken? Then he was taking her with him.

He didn't let her come until her legs were shaking and she was chanting his name like a prayer. Only then did he bring her over, using fingers and tongue to give her what she needed. She came so hard he had to help steady her, forcing him to stay on his knees until he was sure she wouldn't slide to the floor when he let go.

His cock was throbbing in time to his heartbeat, and he was half out of his mind with the need to bury himself inside her. He slipped her leg off his shoulder and came to his feet in one fluid motion, lifting her with him as he stood.

She fastened her arms around his neck and hung on, laughing. "I definitely like you better this way."

"You shouldn't.

Bobbi leaned in until their mouths were almost touching, her next words fanning across his cheeks. "I'm not afraid of you, Sabre."

"You should be." He kissed her hard, pushing her head back against the bulkhead as her nails raked across the back of his neck. He reached between them, positioning himself at her entrance as he braced his legs wider.

He took her with one slow, steady thrust, not stopping until he was buried balls deep inside her. She moaned into his mouth, the slick heat of her channel pulsing around his cock. He should have waited, given her time to adjust, but he didn't. He took her hard and fast. When it came to Bobbi, he had no control.

As if sensing his thoughts, she broke their kiss and leaned back to stare at him, her dark eyes wide and filled with a wild fire he wanted to bask in forever. Her heels dug into his ass on his next thrust, driving him deeper still.

"Tell me what you want," he demanded.

"More." She flexed her body around his cock, milking him hard. "All of it. All of you. Please, Kurt. Show me who you really are."

He couldn't have denied her request even if he'd wanted to. He was too far gone now. He powered into her, each thrust coming harder than the one before. The scent of sex filled his mouth and nose, the sounds of their lovemaking echoing around the cabin.

"Yes!" she closed her eyes, shuddering as her orgasm started.

He watched her come. Felt her fly apart in his arms, the power of her orgasm pushing him over the edge and into his own release. He barely felt the sting of her nails on his back as he emptied himself into her with her name on his lips.

He leaned in and kissed her, slow and soft this time. When he raised his head again, she was smiling up at him, her hand on his cheek. "Hey, handsome."

"Hey, beautiful. You okay?"

"So much more than okay." She moved her hand to smooth away the furrow between his brows. "Stop worrying about me. It's sweet but unnecessary. I trust you. Hell, I'm probably safer here with you than anywhere else in the galaxy."

"You'd be safer back at Astek Station."

"I don't think so. You're my safe space. Where you go, I follow."

He didn't bother pulling out of her. He just gathered her into his arms and walked her to the nearest couch, sitting them both down so she was astride his thighs. "That's not going to work, minx."

"Hmmm?" She gave him a lazy, pleased smile.

"Pushing my buttons. I'm too relaxed for that to work right now."

"Then I guess I'll just have to try again later."

He chuckled as she burrowed into his arms, her head on his chest. "You do that, and we're going to end up back here again."

She pressed a kiss to his bare chest. "That's what I'm hoping for."

He closed his eyes and bowed his head over hers. "Stars save me, Erben was right. I did join his damned club."

"What club is that?"

"The one for guys who fall for dangerous women. You, little minx, are the most dangerous woman I've ever met." And now he'd had a taste of her passion and felt the heat of her fire, Kurt had no intentions of letting her go—not now and maybe not ever.

Veth. He was in so much trouble.

10

She was seated beside Kurt, both of them squeezed into the small amount of space behind Archer's desk, watching a screen so large it felt like they were chatting to his team through an open window despite the fact they were on separate ships.

She'd suggested she sit in his lap for this meeting, but she'd only been teasing. Even after spending most of their time naked and tangled up with each other, all it took was a touch and they'd be at it again. Definitely not something the rest of his team needed to see.

"Still nothing?" Kurt asked.

It was the first time she'd seen the rest of Team Three's faces since before the gala. The only one missing was Dante. She assumed he was flying the ship, milking it for every bit of speed he could wring from her engines. The others all showed signs of fatigue and worry. She knew how they felt. They were all concerned, which was why they were having this meeting in real time instead of sticking to short, encrypted bursts that would be harder to detect.

Dax shook his head. "It's like the whole area and every ship in it fell into a black hole. It's been a full day now, and no one has been able to make contact. IAF ships from all over the sector are making best speed for the Drift, but they have no estimate of when they'll get there. Colonel Bahl has sent Team Four to investigate. They'll be there in fifty hours or so."

"You're closer. You could turn the *Malora* around..." Kurt started to say, but Dax cut him off with a gesture.

"Our orders are to hunt down Clooney and bring him back for interrogation."

"And retrieve whatever Lange gave him," Bobbi said. She needed to stay focused on the plan. Every time she stopped, she started worrying about her uncle and everyone back on Astek. Tianna and her husbands. Private Reddy, Irani, and the girl's boisterous poly family. Bobbi couldn't do anything to help them. Hell, she'd taken the *Bat*, leaving Scott without his emergency escape plan. A surge of guilt welled up, but she pushed it back down and forced herself to tune in to what was being said.

"Any luck figuring out what that might have been?" Eric asked from his spot at the table. "It doesn't make sense that they'd do a physical handoff if it was just data. It had to be something tangible."

"But small." Bobbi sketched out the approximate size of the object with her hands.

"Bio-weapon sample, maybe?" Aria suggested.

"Possible," Dax agreed.

"Or stolen tech," Eric said.

"Also possible, but we've got no way to confirm any of these theories right now. The answers are back at Astek station, and we can't talk to them."

Kurt leaned forward and steepled his hands on the desk. "So, what *are* we here to talk about, sir?"

"Our orders." Dax looked around the table and then directly at Kurt. "You're not going to like them."

"You know I hate it when you get dramatic, sir."

Cris laughed and held out a hand to Eric. "Told you. Pay up."

Aria shook her head. "When I suggested you get a new hobby, your lordship, gambling wasn't what I had in mind."

Cris froze. Only for a second, but Bobbi saw it. Then he carried on, joking and laughing as if nothing had happened. "I considered knitting, but this is way more profitable. Besides, we both know I've never been good at taking your advice, Blink."

Aria opened her mouth to reply, but Dax rapped his knuckles on the table, drawing their attention back to him. "You all need to hear this, so listen up."

There was no mistaking his words for anything other than what they were. An order. He didn't command the same way her uncle did, but the effect was the same. Everyone turned their attention to him, her included.

"He's good," she murmured so softly only Kurt could hear her.

"He's the best." Kurt took her hand in his and squeezed it.

"Two minutes, sir," Eric called out.

Dax grimaced. "Looks like you two are getting the short and brutal version. Lieutenant Commander Castille, you are hereby seconded to Nova Force Team Three for the duration of this mission. You will get your orders from me or Lieutenant Commander Meyer. Welcome to the team."

Bobbi managed not to cheer, but she couldn't keep the grin off her face. She was in! "Yes, sir."

Kurt smacked the desk with an open hand. "What? Why? This is a dangerous mission, sir, and she's not trained for this kind of thing."

"Then you have two days to get her up to speed. We're alone out here, Sabre, and whether you like it or not, Castille is an IAF officer. We use the tools we have on hand. That includes Castille. Operation Artemis is over."

"Castille might be an officer, but she's also Archer's niece. He gave me very clear orders about her, sir."

"I'm aware. But you're forgetting something. We don't answer to Archer. If he has a problem with Colonel Bahl's orders, he can take it up with her."

"I don't like it."

"Noted. Do it anyway." And there it was again, that note of command.

Kurt snapped to attention. Or as close to it as he could manage while sitting down. "Yes, sir."

Bobbi did her best to hide her elation from Kurt. She knew he'd follow Dax's orders, but he wouldn't be happy about it. He and her uncle were on the same page when it came to the outdated notion that she needed their protection. She would just have to make him see the truth. Tactfully, of course. She loved pushing his buttons when it came to their personal lives, but this was something different. It was the one area she'd agreed to listen to him, and she intended to keep her word.

"Thirty seconds, sir," Eric called out again.

"One more thing."

"Sir?" she and Kurt said at the same time.

"This whole mission is time sensitive. The sooner we grab Clooney, the faster we can get back to Astek and find out what happened to our friends."

Kurt grimaced. "You don't want us to wait for you." It was a statement, not a question.

"You'll have to use your best judgment once we know where our target is going. If you need us, wait. I'm not going to ask you to risk your lives for no good reason. But if there is any way you can do this mission on your own, you need to do so."

"Understood."

Dax rapped his knuckles on the table again. "Good hunting, my friend. We'll be in touch."

There was a quick moment of mutual goodbyes, and then the screen went blank.

Kurt sat back in his chair, head back, eyes closed as if he were in pain. "You can celebrate now."

She bounced out of her chair, raised both hands in the air and yelled, "Yes!"

Kurt cracked open one eye to watch her, his lips twitching. "Feel better now?"

She beamed. She was officially part of this thing

now—not an outsider but one of the team. When she got back, she'd have to thank Colonel Bahl for giving her the chance. She'd become a lawyer because she wanted to make a difference, but this was an opportunity to do more than she could ever do in a courtroom. "Oh yeah. I feel awesome!" Then something occurred to her. "What the hell was Operation Artemis?"

He looked slightly sheepish. "Originally? *You* were. Well, you and Archer. Eventually the whole team was read in and the mission was expanded to hunt for any and all moles inside the IAF."

"How many of them knew I was under investigation?" she asked softly.

"Just me, Dax, and Trinity. The rest might have guessed, but by the time they did, I was pretty sure neither of you were spies."

She skewered him with a look. "As if Uncle Scott would turn traitor. He'd die first. At least I got a wicked sounding code name. Artemis. Greek goddess of the hunt, right?"

"And chastity," he pointed out in an oh-so-casual tone.

She laughed. "Lucky for you that last bit doesn't work for me. Still, badass nickname or not, I'm glad we're past all that. You investigating me while I was investigating all of you was pretty much the definition of paranoia."

He snorted. "And a waste of time, though. I will bet you a whole tray of that caviar stuff you like that Archer never admits to that."

"No bet." She cocked her head. "You're taking this rather well. Do you need to yell too? I know having me along wasn't what you wanted."

"Plans change. Plus, I can't complain about the company." He winked. "I don't need to yell, but I could use an hour or so with a heavy bag. I don't suppose this ship has a gym?"

"Lower deck, in the stern. It's not a big space, but most of what you need is stashed in compartments in the walls and floor. Tell Boo what you need and it will set it up for you." Bobbi let her voice drop to a seductive whisper and then walked her fingers up his chest. "Or, I could help you work off some of that negative energy some other way…"

He caught her hand and held it. "Tempting, but maybe later. First, you and I need to start your training. I've already inventoried the weapons locker. What do you know about plasma grenades?"

"They go boom?" She was certified for most firearms, but that was the extent of her training. JAG officers weren't expected to go into combat. Their battles were fought in courtrooms, not the field.

"Technically correct, but a little light on the details. We've got two days and a whole lot of information to cover."

"I'm ready. I'll listen. I'll learn. I'm not going to do anything that could get me killed."

He raised her hand to his mouth and kissed her fingers. "That's not what I'm worried about."

She cocked her head and laughed. "Liar."

"Okay, that's not *all* I'm worried about." His

expression was serious, but the look in his eyes hit her hardest. She saw concern there, a lot of it.

"What else?"

"If you make a mistake down there, your life isn't the only one on the line. I can't protect you if I'm dead."

His words stung. "I will be the best student you've ever had. I will not screw up."

"Yes, you will. Because it's your first time, and some things only experience can teach you. So, prepare yourself for that, Bobbi. You will make mistakes."

She nodded. "Okay." She was determined to prove him wrong, but that didn't mean she'd disregard his warning.

He stared at her so intently she felt like he was peering into her soul. In a way, he was. He was reading her, and this time she allowed it without any attempt to mask her feelings. "I'm not a fool, Kurt. If we go after Clooney, I will follow your orders." She took a breath and then added, "And you don't need to worry too much about me getting hurt. I know you and the rest of the team were offered the medi-bot treatment. I already accepted that same offer."

He was on his feet a split second later, staring down at her with an expression she couldn't decipher. Was it horror? Anger? Shock?

"Who the *fraxx* thought giving you access to nanotech was a good idea?"

"Do you really need to ask?"

He pinched the bridge of his nose and groaned. "Archer."

"Got it in one."

"I suppose this means he's got them, too? Which is probably a good thing. It means whatever is going on back on the Drift, he's got a good chance of surviving it."

She didn't hide the impact of his words. She was done keeping secrets from him. It might not be the easiest way to start a relationship, but it was the only way to get through the mission. "That's what I keep telling myself."

He winced. "Sorry. I'll get my foot out of my mouth, now."

"It's okay. Until yesterday you didn't know he was my family. You've got friends back there, too. And Dante must be out of his mind not knowing what's happened to his girlfriend and their adopted son. They're still on Astek aren't they?"

"Yeah." Kurt exhaled sharply. "And Dante will be worried sick, but he knows Tyra and Nico are tough and smart. Hell, Nico was a street kid before Dante found him. I wouldn't be surprised if we come back and discover the kid has laid claim to a food court somewhere and named himself the King of Burgerland."

"Burgerland?" she asked.

"I'll tell you all about it later. Right now, I need to know about you. How long ago did you have the treatment? What benefits have you experienced? I need to know everything." He frowned. "Wait. Is this why you thought you could go after Clooney alone? Because of the medi-bots?"

"Well, yeah. When I said I was tougher than you

thought, I meant it." She held out her arm. The one the Pheran had clawed. "I injected myself the first day of the party. After that asshole attacked me, this healed on its own. In fact, the wounds were already closing up before we left. By the next morning it was like it never happened."

"Bet it still hurt like a bitch, though."

"It did. And I know what you're going to say next. Accelerated healing won't save me from a blaster bolt to the head. Pain is still pain. And no matter how much better my body functions now, it still has limits." She lowered her arm and then took his hand. "I get that. I do."

"Yet you went after Clooney alone." He gripped her hand tightly. "You can't do that again."

"I won't. I don't have to this time. I've got you and the rest of the team now. I'm not doing this on my own anymore."

He folded her into his arms and buried his face in her hair. "You are definitely not alone, little minx."

She melted at his touch, the now familiar rush of heat and desire filling her veins. That wasn't all she felt, though. There was more. Comfort, a soul-deep sense of rightness she'd never felt with anyone else. She closed her eyes and let herself bask in the feeling. If she hadn't taken the risks she had, she might have missed out on all of this.

Some things were worth taking chances for.

～

Kurt breathed in the subtle scent of her hair and tried to think of a way to get around his orders. Bobbi wasn't ready for this. He could teach her weapons and tactics, sure. That was the easy part. Teaching her to be part of a team... that wasn't so simple. It was a problem he'd experienced recently with Nyx. The former assassin was still working to integrate fully with the rest of the team, and she had the advantage of drilling with them day after day.

Bobbi was a lawyer, not a field operative. He couldn't build on her experience to help guide her through this because she didn't have any. Nor did she understand what it might cost her if she had to kill someone.

Enemy or not, ending someone's life came with a price. Even if he could protect her body, he couldn't shield her from the potential damage to her soul. No, she wouldn't be safe if she came with him, and he needed her safe and whole. Not because Archer ordered him to but because of what she meant to him.

She was the only woman who pushed back when he growled and deliberately punched his buttons just so she could watch his control shatter. She wasn't afraid of the darkness he carried inside him. He wasn't sure yet if that was a good thing or not, but he wanted to stay with her long enough to find out. To do that, he had to keep them both alive. Which wouldn't be easy when she was used to operating alone, and her new infusion of medi-bots gave her a dangerous sense of invulnerability.

What the hell had Archer been thinking dragging Bobbi into this? The colonel had brought his niece to

Astek and dropped her into the middle of a high-stakes investigation with no support. Then, he'd offered Bobbi a life-changing treatment and left her to deal with the consequences alone. Hell, she'd casually stated she injected *herself* with the nanotech. No doctor. No one there to make sure nothing went wrong. When he got back to Astek, he planned on having a few words with the colonel about the way he'd used Bobbi. She deserved better—not just from her uncle but from her commanding officer.

"So, honesty time. How pissed are you that you've been ordered to take me with you?"

He stayed still and quiet for a few more seconds, aware that once he spoke, things could change between them. "I'm not angry. I understand the logic behind the order."

"But?" She pulled out of his arms and then stepped back so she could look up at him without craning her neck. Her expression was calm, but he recognized the storm brewing in her eyes.

"But if there's a way to keep you out of this, I will take it."

"Dammit, Kurt. Don't shut me out."

Something in her words caught at his heart and pulled. "Hey. I'm not doing that. You're still part of the team."

She took another step back. "How do you figure that? You just said you're going to do everything you can to leave me behind."

"No, I said if there was a way to keep you out of harm's way, I'd take it. Which means you'd be coordinating things from the ship. Tracking Clooney, working with local law enforcement, relaying info to the *Malora*."

Her expression softened slightly, but she didn't look convinced. "I could do that."

"We've got two days to cover all the contingencies. Fido told me to get you up to speed, and that's what I'm going to do. It all depends on what Clooney does next. He could stop at one of two colonized planets. If he flies past them, we're into wild space. We're going to need multiple plans."

"We will." She smiled softly. "I like the sound of that. We. Us. That's all I want."

Words he hadn't intended to say tumbled out of his mouth. "Me too. Whatever happens in the next few days, I'm hoping there will still be an us when this is over."

Half a second later she was back in his arms, all joy, sass, and light again. "Did you just ask me to go steady, Lieutenant Commander Meyer?"

"Apparently." He cupped her cheek in one hand, letting his thumb sweep across the soft curve of her lips. Need coiled deep in his belly. He wanted her again. It didn't matter that they'd spent half their waking hours making love, or that he'd taken her in the shower not twenty minutes before their meeting. His need for her was a constant thing, and now that he knew her taste and the way her voice rose at the moment of orgasm, he just wanted her more.

"If I say yes, are you going to take that as permission to boss me around?"

"That is a possibility." He bowed his head and brushed a gentle kiss to her mouth. "But we both know I'm going to boss you around either way. And either way, you kind of like it."

"Says who?" Her words were defiant, but he didn't miss the shiver that ran through her, or the way she licked her lips before she spoke.

"Says me." He kissed her before she could say anything else, though he felt her growl of annoyance vibrate on his tongue. She wasn't the only one who knew how to push buttons.

Soft hands slid under his borrowed T-shirt, tempting him to forget all about their need to train and make plans. All he wanted to do was strip her out of the shapeless shipsuit and take her up against the nearest flat surface. Horizontal or vertical, he didn't care which.

It took all the will power he had left to break their kiss and let the demands of reality push their way back into his awareness.

"Pushy jerk," she muttered, but she was smiling as she said it.

"Stubborn minx."

She smirked. "And you kind of like me that way."

Hell yeah. She made him crazy in ways he never imagined, and he liked it a lot. Probably more than was wise, given they were a few short days away from a mission with so many unknowns. How the hell did Dax manage to balance the demands of the job against the safety of the woman he loved?

Kurt's heart stuttered. *Love?* Oh *fraxx*, no. Where had

that thought come from and how did he make it go away? He was not in love with Bobbi... was he?

His head rattled off a list of reasons why that couldn't happen. It was too soon. The timing was wrong. It was just lust masquerading as something more. His heart paid no attention to his brain and gave another answer. *Yes.*

For a moment, he forgot how to breathe. He loved her. When the *fraxx* had that happened? His arms tightened around her, crushing her against him until she made a soft squawk of protest.

"Ribs."

"Sorry." He kissed the top of her head and then grudgingly let her go. "As much as I would like to spend some time showing you just how much I like your sass, we have work to do. I'm going to need to make some training notes. While I do that, I need you to familiarize yourself with the clothing fabricator. I can't keep raiding your uncle's closet, and shipsuits might not be practical wherever we wind up. Find out what the fabricator's limitations are and then start making basic outfits for both of us. Tear resistant fabrics. Pockets. Layers."

"Got it."

"I'll come find you when I'm done." He kissed her again and then tapped her on the ass. "Move it."

She stuck out her tongue at him. "Moving it, sir." Her salute was more of an obscene gesture as she walked out of the small office, leaving him alone.

He sank back into his chair and blew out a long breath. He picked up his comm unit from the desk and tapped out a brief message to his commander. It was just one word, but he knew Dax would understand it.

"Advice?"

While he waited, he started drafting up a training plan for Bobbi. Training new team members was part of his duties, but he'd never had to cover so much in so little time. He was still making notes when Dax's answer came through.

"Accept that the best way to keep her safe is to train her well. Oh, and make sure you don't piss her off because while she's covering your ass, she'll be perfectly positioned to shoot you in it. Good luck. Welcome to the club."

He read it and then barked out a short riff of laughter. He really needed to find someone else to go to for relationship advice.

11

BOBBI STARED AT THE VIEWSCREEN. It showed several lush, green continents grouped together near the equator of the relatively normal-looking planet. What wasn't normal were the vast array of red warning lights blinking urgently all around the perimeter of the screen. A lot of it was scrolling by too fast for her to read, but she caught enough to grasp that the planet they were orbiting had had plenty of lifeforms living on it, and apparently many of them were dangerous to humans.

According to the official records, this entire system was owned by Black Rock Mining Ltd and was completely uninhabited. It didn't even have a name, just a string of numbers and letters. Clooney clearly knew something the records didn't because he'd dropped into normal space just outside the system and made straight for the planet, landing next to a manmade structure that was also missing from the official records.

"Guess we can officially put Black Rock in the

Grays' camp. Huh?" she asked, still scanning through the rapidly scrolling warnings.

"They're either complicit, incompetent, or more likely, both. We see this a lot. It only takes one or two senior executives making a few careful changes and suddenly shipping companies have missing inventory, mining corporations lose track of a planet or two, and money gets moved around. The next thing you know, someone's carved out a new kingdom for themselves with no one the wiser. I'll bet if we dig deep enough, we'll discover this company is a shell for one of the bigger corporations, too."

"And no one stops this from happening?" As a lawyer, she spent her life dealing with beings looking to make the laws work in their favor, but the idea that some people were stealing whole planets… it was hard to wrap her head around.

"We stop them. That's why Nova Force exists." Kurt looked over at her. "Do you want to hear the whole recruitment speech? It's long but has some good bits."

"Nope. No need. I've already been recruited. Remember?" She kept her words light, but no way would either of them forget that little fact. How could they when they'd spent nearly every waking moment of the last four days getting her ready? Weapons. Tactics. Basic survival training. Most of it was theoretical of course, but Kurt had made her field strip her weapons so many times she dreamed about it now, and he'd taken her down to the little gym and given her a crash course in self-defense that would have left her battered and bruised if it weren't for her medi-bots.

"Temporarily," he reminded her. "One mission only." He pointed to the screen. "Do you want the good news or the bad news first?"

There was bad news? He wasn't going to keep her on the ship. Was he? Not after she'd worked so hard. "Good news first, please."

"The good news is, you're getting your wish. The rest of the team is still more than a day away. We can't wait for them, and the terrain is too hostile for me to go alone."

She kept her expression carefully neutral, but inside she was doing mental handsprings. She was in! "And the bad news?"

"The bad news is you're getting your wish."

She scowled. "How is that also the bad news?"

"Hostile terrain. Hell, hostile everything. We are going to be dropping into the middle of a dense rainforest with only what we can carry to sustain us."

"Why into the rainforest?"

He tapped the viewscreen, zooming in on the area around where Clooney had landed. "That is the only safe landing site within several hundred kilometers. So, we're going to have to trek in from outside reasonable sensor range and hope like hell he doesn't have the ability to detect a stealthed ship."

"And if he does?"

He pressed his hands together and then moved them apart, fingers outstretched. "Boom. Bye-bye *Bat*."

"I'm going to go on the record as stating I'm not a fan of that outcome."

"Me either. So, we'll do everything we can to avoid

attracting attention. We can't do deep scans, but it doesn't look like there are underground structures or anywhere to hide another ship, so we can assume he's alone down there."

"Unless that's a manned base?" she suggested.

"If it is, I pity whoever drew that duty. You're right, though, we shouldn't assume anything." He stared at the screen, but his eyes were distant and unfocused.

She'd learned enough about him in the last few days to know he was working out a plan. She'd also learned to leave him alone when he got like this. She left the cockpit and took the stairs down to the lower level. They'd be traversing a rainforest, which meant she needed to fabricate waterproof gear to go with the basic items already packed and ready. The climate was warm and humid, the local wildlife hostile, and if she'd read the warnings right, even some of the plant life was potentially dangerous. "Boo. Show me everything you can fabricate suitable for our needs based on the mission specs Lieutenant Commander Bossyboots mentioned a few minutes ago in the cockpit."

"Do you wish me to continue referring to our guest by that name? He has repeatedly informed me his surname is Meyer."

"No change. Please disregard his requests." It was petty and childish, and she giggled every time the AI used the name she'd assigned him that first day on board. The time for games and giggles was ending. She knew that. The moment they started their descent, everything would change. It had already started. The wild passion and laughter of their first night had been replaced with hours of intense instruction and drills. They still had moments, and when they tumbled into bed each night the sex had been incredible, but she felt like something was missing. Maybe it would come back after this mission was over. *Or maybe what we have wasn't meant to last.*

She didn't want to believe that, but it wouldn't be the first time. She'd learned the hard way not to rush into a relationship. It saved heartache later, when things didn't work out. She hadn't done that with Kurt. She'd fallen for him despite all the reasons she shouldn't have... or maybe because of them. Forbidden fruit was always the most tempting. Right? Toss in some danger, adrenaline, and then garnish with a cherry by locking them up alone on a ship for a few days. It was inevitable they'd hook up. She didn't want that to be all there was, though. She wanted more for herself. More for them. But that would have to wait. For now, she needed to stay focused on the mission.

She had most of their stuff fabricated and packed by the time he joined her. He was wearing enough weaponry to start a small war with a bag of what looked like more weapons slung over one shoulder.

"You're changed already. Good. Gear up. We'll be starting our descent soon. I've sent a message to the *Malora*." He handed her the bag, and she grunted in surprise at the weight of it.

"Did you leave anything behind?"

He winked. "I couldn't figure out a way to bring the rocket launcher. Too big."

"If we die because we weren't prepared to take out something the size of a ship, I'm blaming you."

She was already wearing tactical webbing over her clothes, and it didn't take her long to get everything transferred from the bag to her body. They'd drilled on this too. She knew the name and purpose of every item she carried and where to find it, right down to the garrote woven under her collar. They hadn't been able to find body armor to fit her, so she was going without.

He stripped off the lightweight ship suit he'd been wearing and put on the clothing she'd fabricated for him, along with a lightly armored tactical vest he'd found in her uncle's closet.

As often as she'd seen him naked now, she still paused to admire the view. The grace in his movements reminded her of the night they'd danced together. Watching the play of muscle and sinew beneath his skin made her fingers itch to touch him, to trace every etched line of his body and count every scar. She jammed her hands into the pockets of her pants instead.

"I forgot to check. What's the gravity on this world?" she asked once she had everything in place. "Am I going to be able to move wearing all this gear?"

"You are. Gravity is about ninety percent of standard. Oxygen is slightly less than normal, though, so don't push yourself too hard. We're going to have to watch for heat exhaustion and dehydration too."

"Next time, we book with a different travel agent."

He chuckled. "How about we stay home instead?"

"What? And give up all this glamor and excitement?" She gestured around them and then to herself. She was dressed exactly like he was. Both of them in olive green pants made from the sturdiest fabric they had on board. They had long-sleeve shirts of the same fabric, worn over simple black tank tops. The boots had been the trickiest part. Her uncle hadn't considered the possibility that someone with a far smaller foot size might need shoes made, so she'd had to experiment, cutting things down by hand until she found a design that worked.

He stalked over to her, grabbed her by the webbing, and hauled her in for a kiss so hot she wondered if they'd leave scorch marks on the floor. That thought fled, leaving her operating on instinct and need, both of which screamed at her to hold on tightly and never let him go. She tangled one hand in his tactical rig and threw her arm around his waist, pulling herself in so close she could feel the heat of his body even through all their clothing. His cock was a steel bar pressing into her stomach as their tongues danced, an entire conversation about wants, worries, and needs all compressed into a brief moment of raw physical contact.

"Hello, Roberta and Lieutenant Commander Bossyboots. As per your request I am providing you with a two-minute warning before I begin my descent. I suggest you both return to the main cabin and strap in. The transition to atmospheric flight is often rough."

Boo's calm voice snapped her out of the lust-fueled fog she was in. It seemed to do the same for Kurt because he raised his head with a frustrated snarl. "On our way."

He let go of her, and a moment later he was snapping something around her waist. "What?" She looked down and then back up at him. "Why am I wearing a suspension belt?"

"You're not. That is an anti-grav harness. Think of it as a suspension belt's big brother. Same concept, only these can generate stronger fields for a much longer time frame. I apologize for not covering this in your training. I wasn't expecting to use them. Hell, I wasn't aware there were any on board. It's not a common piece of equipment. As for why you're wearing it? I'll explain once we're strapped in."

He grabbed their packs, took one last look around the area they'd used for mission prep, and then nodded. "Time to head upstairs."

She followed him through the ship and up the stairs, chatting as she went. "Uncle Scott likes to be prepared for any scenario. The Bat is basically his personal bunker." She sighed. "And I took it just when he could have used it the most. I hope there's nothing here he needs to deal with whatever is going on back at Astek."

Kurt glanced back over his shoulder at her. "He has an entire base full of weapons and equipment at his disposal. I know you're worried about him, but Archer is not the kind to go down easily. I will bet you a triple chocolate sundae with extra cherries that by the time we get back he's got everything under control. He'll be waiting for us at the dock, wanting to know if you and the *Bat* came through unscathed and ready to kick my ass if there's a scratch on either one of you."

"Then it's a good thing I heal fast. Given you just put me in an anti-grav harness and won't tell me why."

"It's a surprise."

"Wait. Is this revenge for me showing up at the party without warning you I was coming?"

The grin he flashed her was almost feral. "Maybe."

Her heart was racing as she took her seat. She didn't know if the danger or Kurt was the cause, but if she had to make a guess, she'd bet it was the man, not the mission.

While they waited, Kurt showed Bobbi how to use the controls on her harness. Most of the functions would happen automatically, but she needed to know how to override the system if something went wrong.

"So, we're just going to jump out the rear door and float down to the planet?" She gave him an incredulous look from her seat across from him. "That's your whole plan?"

"That's my new and improved plan. The first version had us rapelling from the ship to the ground by ropes. Not easy to do through the dense tree canopy like we're dealing with here. This will be easier. Oh, and I would advise against jumping out the door. That will change your trajectory. Cross your arms over your chest and then step off like you were going down a flight of stairs. Once you're in the air, keep your legs together and try to thread your body through the canopy as best you can. Protect your face and try not to get hung up on anything."

"You make it sound simple." For the first time, there was a hint of worry in her eyes. He was happy to see it. It meant she was aware of the danger they faced. That awareness might make all the difference down there. In his years of service, he'd learned that a little fear could be a good thing. Too much could cripple a soldier, but a lack of fear was just as dangerous. She'd already proven she had a reckless streak. Concern would temper those impulses. At least, he hoped so.

"Remember what we talked about? If something feels too complex, you break it down into smaller bits until it seems simple. So, first we jump. Then we float. Then we land."

"Only we don't jump. We step."

"See? You got this." He reached out and gripped her hand. "If I didn't think you could do this, your ass would not leave this ship. I would tie you to a damned chair and leave you here cursing a blue streak."

Her brows rose, and a smile touched the edges of her mouth. "You would. Wouldn't you?"

"Without hesitation."

She blew out a breath. "Okay. So. We're doing this."

"Yes we are." He let go of her hand. He needed to stop thinking of her as someone he cared about and start seeing her as his partner on this mission. He'd done all he could to prepare her. Now, he needed to trust her to do her job so he could do his.

"Just step off!" He had to yell to be heard over the engine's roar. He was standing to Bobbi's left, just inside the door. Bobbi was geared up and ready to go, her toes hanging over the edge of the open doorway, arms crossed over her chest and her face slightly ashen. "Why am I going first?" she shouted back.

"Because if I went first, there'd be no one around to push you."

Her eyes went wide. "You wouldn't!"

He cocked his head and arched a brow.

She hesitated for another second and then sighed and stepped out into the open air, flipping him off with both hands as she drifted toward the ground.

Five seconds later, he stepped out after her.

The heat was stifling, the air so humid it felt like he was trying to breathe steam. He was sweating only seconds after leaving the ship and he knew it would only get worse once they dropped below the canopy.

He couldn't see the ship now that he was outside it, but he could tell by the change in the engine's noise that it was on the move. They were on their own until the *Malora* arrived.

He glanced down in time to see Bobbi reach the upper canopy of the forest. He watched as she vanished into the mass of green like she was being swallowed whole. A few seconds later her voice was in his ear. "Watch for thorns on your way down. The branches bite."

"You hurt?"

"Minor scrapes. Nothing to worry about."

"Anything else I should know?"

"It's *fraxxing* hot in here. Also, I had no idea there were this many shades of green. Otherwise, all good. See you soon."

He managed to don a pair of heavy gloves before his feet reached the canopy. She was right about the thorns. They tore at his clothes and snagged on his harness. He had to twist and fight to keep free of them. The gloves protected him from the worst of it, but he was still scratched and bleeding by the time he touched down.

Bobbi already had her first aid kit open. "We need to disinfect your cuts before we get going. This place is a living petri dish full of stars know what kind of nasty bugs your immune system has no defense against."

When she turned to face him, he noted she had a smear of blood along one cheek. But the cut it had come from had already healed, leaving nothing but a thin pink line. "I wasn't sure I wanted to take the medi-bot treatment, but now I'm seeing the benefits, I'm going to have to rethink things."

She laughed. "It's all a matter of perspective. Sure, we're changing our life expectancy and altering our bodies on a cellular level. But on the other hand, all the ice cream we can eat for the rest of our lives."

He bitched and groused as she cleaned up his scratches, more for something to say than from any real discomfort. When she was done, she leaned in and pressed a gentle kiss to each injury on his face.

"There, all better."

"Thank you." He wanted to pull her in close and kiss her properly, but he settled for a quick kiss to the tip of her nose. Now wasn't the time for distractions.

They had a job to do first. After that, he had plans for the two of them. A hotel. Room service. No spies to hunt. No life or death decisions. And no AIs that sounded disturbingly like Scott Archer interrupting their alone time.

He caught a flicker of disappointment in her eyes as he got back to his feet, but she didn't say anything as she turned and repacked the first aid kit.

They took a few moments to put away the harnesses and shoulder their packs. Then he consulted the navigation data on his comm unit. "According to this, we need to cover just over ten clicks in that direction. You ready to go?"

"I am. The sooner we start, the sooner we can get out of here." She fanned her face with one hand.

"Heat getting to you?"

"I can deal with the heat. It's the noise. It's doing my head in."

He had to agree with her. The forest was alive with unfamiliar sounds. The buzz of insects was a constant background drone punctuated by clicks, trills, and warbles. Birds, or whatever passed for them on this world, screeched and sang from hidden vantage points all around them, all of it blending together into a constant cacophony of noise too loud to ignore.

"With any luck, it'll die down once I start clearing a path through that." He pointed toward the wall of brush, trees, and roots that blocked their path.

"This really works?"

"It does. Good thing, too. If we had to clear this by hand we'd be out here for days." He drew a blaster and reset the controls so it emitted a low intensity, wide-angle beam. Then, he aimed it at the brush and pulled the trigger. The plant life browned, withered, and then burned away, leaving a path wide enough for them to walk through. The ground steamed slightly beneath their feet and the scent of scorched wood was thick in the air as they moved to the end of the cleared section and started the process again. As an added benefit, it dealt with some of the more unpleasant wildlife lurking out of sight. He hadn't been able to learn if there were snakes on this planet, but he wasn't taking any chances.

Two hours later, they'd depleted the charge on one blaster and were taking turns cutting the path with two others. Rotating helped prevent the power packs from overheating. He'd forgotten how fast heat and humidity *fraxxed* with equipment.

"I've been in space too long," he muttered, swiping the sweat out of his eyes with the back of his sleeve.

"Climate-controlled and bug-free living. Yeah. Sign me up." She flicked something with a multitude of legs off her pants with a grimace. "How much farther?"

"We're over halfway. What say we clear this last section and then break for food and water?"

"Sounds good." She moved past him and raised her blaster, following the same pattern they'd been doing for hours. Only this time, something new happened.

The trees in front of them went up in flames like they'd been doused in rocket fuel, and then the damned things exploded.

12

BOBBI HAD BEEN EXPECTING WEIRDNESS. They were on an alien planet, after all. The gravity was wrong. The air was too thin. Everything around her was unfamiliar. She'd coped with everything this hellhole had thrown at her, but she hadn't been prepared for exploding trees.

"What the *fraxx*!" she yelled as the flames rushed skyward. She barely had time to turn away from the fire before a series of small, staccato explosions ripped through the air. She dove for the ground, expecting to get torn up by shrapnel any second. She looked up from the dirt, hoping to get one last look at Kurt before the end.

He was face down on the ground less than two meters away, hands over his head, but then…nothing else happened. Sparks and burning debris filled the air, sizzling as it hit the ground around them. There were a few more sporadic explosions, like the last few fireworks at the end of a festival, and then the forest was blissfully silent.

Kurt surged to his feet the moment it quieted and scrambled over to her. He was covered in half-rotted leaves, mud, and ash from the plants they'd burned away. "Bobbi!"

"Singed and confused, but still here." She pushed herself to a sitting position and looked around, not entirely sure why she was still alive. The flames were dying down now. The fire hadn't been able to spread far because everything was so damp and humid. The flash point had been a stand of tall, skinny trees clumped tightly together. The fire had burned away all their leaves and left them smoldering and blackened in the middle of the path.

She looked up and noticed the air was thick with what looked like ash at first, but after a moment, she realized it was something else. Seeds floated in the sultry air, each drifting beneath a delicate sail of some kind of fluffy plant-matter.

"What in the hell…" she trailed off and settled for just pointing wordlessly upward.

Kurt pulled her into his arms and held her close, hands moving over her carefully. "You're sure you're not hurt? You were standing right in front of the blast."

"I think I got a few sparks in my hair, but that's it. I'm okay." She covered one of his hands with hers. "I'm really okay. Are you?"

"When we get back to the ship, I am going to need to gargle with something fresh and minty for an hour or two to get the taste of jungle rot out of my mouth, but no real harm done. And I have no idea what the *fraxx* happened. Did your blaster malfunction?"

"I don't think so." She handed it over to him, careful to keep the barrel pointed away from them both.

He did a quick inspection but then shook his head. "It's fine."

"And yet, the trees went *kaboom*. I don't recall randomly exploding plant life being on the list of things that could potentially kill us. Then again, it was a long list. Maybe I missed it."

"Nope. Nothing about incendiary trees. We'll have to make a note on it when we get back. Warn the next poor sods who land here." He returned her weapon and then took her face in both hands and stared into her eyes. "I'm glad you're not hurt."

"Same." She went to kiss him, but he was already getting to his feet. Instead of a kiss, she got a hand up. His mixed messages were annoying, but now wasn't the time to call him on it. They had more pressing concerns.

She managed to scrape off the worst of the muck with a stick while Kurt went to inspect the trees.

"Huh." He said a moment later. "I think this is a natural phenomenon."

"There's nothing natural about blaster fire," she pointed out as she joined him.

"Not blaster fire. Regular fire. The kind that happens every time lightning strikes, which I'm betting is pretty often given the climate here."

"Heat response? Like pinecones?" She pointed skyward. "So the explosions were just the seedpods releasing."

"Exactly. And how does a city girl like you know about pinecones?"

"Mamma Celeste grew up on a colony world, one of the older ones that brought over a lot of plants and animals from Earth. Tossing pinecones on the fire was something she and Scott used to do as kids."

"I'm still having trouble envisioning Archer as a kid." Kurt shook his head. "But I think we can keep using the blaster to clear the path. We'll just shorten the beam and try to avoid hitting anymore of the kaboom trees."

"Is that their official name now?"

He grinned, the expression making the fast-drying mud on his face crease and flake. "We discovered them. We get to name 'em."

"I like the way you think. Shall we stick to the plan and take a break now?"

He scrubbed a dirty hand over his equally filthy face and grimaced. "Yeah. And clean up as best we can. I've had immunity boosters and you've got medi-bots, but it's still not a great idea to stay covered in microbes from an unknown ecosystem."

She shuddered. "Ew. While you're gargling away the taste of dirt, I'm going to be taking a very long, very hot shower once we get back."

His eyes gleamed, and for a moment she thought he'd say something about joining her in the shower. But he turned away without saying anything. He used his blaster to clear away a spot at the base of a large tree.

She dropped her pack to the ground and sat down with a contented sigh, her back to the tree.

"You stay here. Rest up. Refuel. I'm going to see if I can find a stream or something where we can wash up."

"Don't go far. Pretty sure things out there are curious to find out what human tastes like."

"They can keep wondering." He didn't bother to burn a path this time, and within seconds he was out of sight, though she could still hear him pushing and swearing his way through the brush.

She broke open one of the food tabs and ate it, washing the dry, tasteless stuff down with water. She was about to open a second one when a large, squishy *something* plopped onto the ground near her feet.

She squawked and scrambled to stand, nearly tripping over the root she'd been sitting on in the process. "Some badass you are," she muttered to herself. Once she was steady on her feet, she took a good look at her unexpected visitor.

It was a lizard. Or something lizard-like. Scales. Tail. Six legs. Big eyes and a flabby, moss-green body that reminded her of a toad. "You fell out of the ugly tree and hit every branch on the way down. Didn't you?"

She glanced up at the tree she'd been sitting under. "Crap. You fell out of *this* tree. Didn't you? Please tell me you were alone up there."

The creature eyed her and then hissed, showing a set of needle-like teeth.

"Shoo." She flapped a hand at it.

It hissed again.

"Don't make me shoot you."

The creature crouched down and spines appeared along its tail. She considered calling for Kurt but didn't.

She'd fought to come on this mission. If she couldn't handle one demon toad with a pissy attitude, she should have stayed on the ship.

She took a slow step backward and drew a blaster. Not the one she'd been using to clear a path but one set to fry anything she shot with it. "Look, I'm sorry I called you ugly. But you really need to go now. If you don't, the trees won't be the only things exploding around here."

It launched itself at her and she fired. At that range, she couldn't have missed if she wanted to. Most of the creature vaporized with a horrific popping sound, and what was left landed on the toe of her boots in a scorched, quivering mass.

"Gah!" She kicked it away out of reflex. "Sorry, little guy. But I warned you."

"I think it's charming that you apologize to the dead. Do you really think it can hear you?"

She spun around as yet another surge of adrenaline hit her overtaxed system. "You!"

The man they'd been chasing for days stood just a few meters away from her, a pulse rifle in his hands with the barrel pointed at her chest. His uniform was immaculate, the shine still on his shoes. He hadn't walked, then. But she hadn't heard anything. How had he gotten to them? How did he even know they were here? Questions and details flooded her mind, distracting her.

Part of her knew she should pull the trigger and shoot him before he shot her, but another part of her mind was playing the death of the demon toad on a loop. She hesitated. Clooney didn't.

Luckily for her, neither did Kurt.

Her lover charged out of the bush, hitting Clooney hard enough his shot went wide. The two men went down in a tangled heap, fists and feet flying. Try as she might, she couldn't get a clean shot on Clooney. They were too close together and moving far too fast.

She holstered her blaster and tried to think. There had to be a way to help. Her hands fluttered as she reached first for a knife and then back for her blaster. What could she do?

While she fought to think clearly, Clooney managed to get the barrel of his rifle across Kurt's throat. Kurt thrashed and bucked to try and free himself, but nothing he did shook the other man loose.

No! She couldn't let this happen. Anger burned away the fog of fear, and in a moment of perfect clarity she knew what she had to do. She fumbled at the collar of her webbing, her fingers scrabbling to find the loops she knew were stitched into the material. As quickly as she could, she circled around behind Clooney. He was staring down at Kurt, muttering something she couldn't make out. It was like he'd forgotten about her, or more likely dismissed her as the lesser threat.

Lesser threat this, asshole. She dropped the garrote over his head, jammed her knee into his back, and pulled with everything she had.

∾

Kurt was losing his battle to stay conscious. His vision was tunneling, and his lungs were burning. He didn't have the energy to kick anymore, and his arms felt like they were made of lead. Where was Bobbi? Was she alright? Had he been too late?

Clooney sneered down at him, his eyes gleaming with malice with his teeth bared in a grim parody of a smile. "Thought you could kick my ass because I'm smaller than you? Think again. The Grays have been generous over the years, and I've had all sorts of interesting upgrades. The best is yet to come, though. After this mission, I'm going digital. I'm going to be immortal and you'll just be dead."

Kurt tried to turn his head to look for Bobbi one last time. He'd faced death too many times to be scared anymore, but he'd be damned if the last thing he saw was Clooney's gloating face. He wanted it to be Bobbi, so he could carry her memory with him into the dark.

She appeared as if he'd summoned her, and for a moment he wondered if she was real or just a near-death hallucination. He got his answer a second later, when she dropped a garrote wire over Clooney's head just the way he'd showed her. He felt a fleeting moment of pride for his student, but it was quickly buried under a tsunami of guilt. He was supposed to be protecting her, not the other way around.

What came next was vicious and ugly, but he didn't look away. Bobbi had made the choice to take a man's life in order to save his. The least he could do was bear witness to the moment she lost part of her soul.

She executed her part perfectly, using her knee to

increase her leverage as she drew the wire tight. Clooney's eyes went wide with pain and terror as he realized what was happening, but by then it was already too late. The wire bit into his flesh, sending a cascade of crimson pouring down his front. Clooney made a gargling wailing noise that ended almost as quickly as it began, the sound sending a fine mist of blood into the air. He reached up with both hands to claw at the wire as he thrashed in incoherent fear.

The moment the pressure was off his neck Kurt sucked in a greedy lungful of air, his chest heaving like a bellows even as he grabbed hold of the pulse rifle in both hands. He protected the trigger area in case Clooney managed one last shot before the end.

He shouldn't have worried. In the time it took him to come back from the brink of unconsciousness, Bobbi had finished the job. As he watched, the light faded from Clooney's eyes while his lifeblood gushed from the gaping wound in his throat.

It took Kurt another few seconds to realize that Bobbi hadn't let go.

"It's okay. He's gone." His voice was little more than a raspy croak, but it was enough to get her attention. She uttered a broken moan and let the body fall to one side.

"Kurt? You're okay? Please be okay." She staggered forward and then dropped to her knees at his side.

"I'm okay." His voice was a little stronger this time, but it was still more of a croak than actual words.

"I...I should have shot him. I could have. I had the chance but I..."

"Shhh. It's over now." He sat up, ignoring the head rush and the pain to gather her into his arms. She was shaking, her breathing jagged and broken by occasional sobs.

Killing someone was never easy. But what she'd done... *Veth*. He held her close and waited for the emotional storm to pass. It didn't take long, and once again he was amazed at her strength and resilience.

Eventually she raised her head and wiped her tears away with one bloody hand. "Well, that sucked vacuum."

"I'm sorry."

She frowned at him. "For what?"

"Leaving you alone. If I'd been here..."

"Then we would have both been distracted by the demonic lizard-toad."

It was his turn to frown. "Explain."

She did. At first it was little more than a jumble of fragmented details, but as she talked, she grew calmer and the story came together.

"So that's why you fired your blaster. That *fraxxing* lizard saved our lives. I heard the shot and came back to check on you."

"Now I feel better *and* worse for shooting it." Bobbi dashed away more tears and then froze, her eyes on her bloodstained hand. "I..." She looked down at herself and then at him with dawning horror, the rest of her words dying away unsaid.

He'd been so focused on her he hadn't even thought about what he must look like. He swiped at his face and his hand came away sticky with blood.

"We're a mess," was all he could think to say.

She laughed, a broken, brittle sound like shards of glass in a burlap sack. He wanted to kiss her, to soothe her any way he could, but he couldn't do that until he wiped away the blood of the man she'd had to kill... because he'd failed to do the job himself.

"That blood. It's his? I mean, you're not hurt?"

He started to shake his head and then stopped as the motion brought fresh pain to his injured throat. "Most of it's his. Some might be mine. Nothing serious."

"You can barely talk, and it looks like your neck is swelling. Let me grab the first aid kit." She pulled away from him before he could argue that he was fine. Before he knew it, she'd taken charge, directing him to join her by their packs. Changing locations also put some distance between them and the body, now mostly concealed by the trunk of the tree.

She handed him a packet of antibacterial wipes and then tore open another one for herself. "First, we get cleaned up. Then you're going to hold still while I do a quick scan. After that I'm going to dose you with some healing accelerant."

He just nodded and followed orders. If she needed to think about something else, he was happy to be the focus of her attention. There would be time enough for both of them to deal with what had just happened, but this wasn't the right time or the right place.

"Where did you learn so much about first aid?" he asked once she'd finished her ministrations.

"Mama Juliana. Every summer we'd take off for two weeks to go camping. No electronics, no communication with the outside world. They taught me all sorts of things on those trips. First aid. Cooking. How to knit. How to play cards." She smiled a little, which was good to see. "How to cheat at cards."

An idea formed in the back of his head. Something to give them both a little time to recover and regroup. After all, with Clooney dead, their mission wasn't urgent anymore. "Did these life lessons include learning how to swim?"

"Of course. Why? Did you come across a nice pool? Maybe with a swim-up bar?"

"No bar. But I did find a place we can get cleaned up. The water is crystal clear, so if anything tries to sneak up and eat us, we'll see it coming."

"Normally, that offer wouldn't tempt me, but…" she shrugged. "Normal left orbit a long time ago. So, swim. Clean up. Finish eating and then what?"

"We finish the mission." He got to his feet, pleased to note that the aches and pains were already fading. "You finish putting that away. I need to check on something."

She gave him a tight look. "You're leaving again?"

"Leaving? No." He jerked his head to indicate the direction of Clooney's body. "I need to check and see what he had on him."

Her cheeks paled a little, but her expression softened. "Right. Do you think he was dumb enough to bring whatever he took out here with him?"

"I'm hoping so, yeah. I mean, he already broke bad guy rule number one."

"There are rules?"

"Oh yeah. I don't remember them all, but no aspiring villain should ever forget the most important ones." He kept up the banter as he moved over to Clooney. The insects were already gathering, rising up in a swarm as he rolled the body over and started his search.

"What's rule number one, then?"

"When you finally meet the heroes in battle, never stop to talk before the fight. And if you insist on doing so, do not, under any circumstances, gloat about your upcoming victory."

She scoffed. "Yeah, he definitely broke that one. He could have shot me before I even knew he was there, but he had to make some pithy remark first. That gave you enough time to tackle him."

"And then he was too busy gloating to me to notice you were coming up behind him." He pulled something smooth and silver out of Clooney's pants pocket and whistled low. "Guess what I found."

"You're kidding. He had it on him?"

"Looks like. Hang on a second, nearly done here."

He finished his search and then gathered up everything he'd found. It wasn't much. There was the pulse rifle, a pocket knife, a comm unit, and a palm-sized, silver box that fit the description Bobbi had given them.

The last thing he did was wipe the blood from his hands before carrying it all back to Bobbi. "Is that it?" he asked her.

"It sure looks like it. Only one way to be sure, though." She touched the clasp but didn't press it.

"Go ahead. You came all this way. Seems fair for you to be the one to open it."

"If this blows up, I'm blaming you."

"He had it in his pants pocket. There's no way he'd keep anything explosive that close to his…" he waved. "You know what I mean."

Her laughter didn't sound broken this time. She opened the container without further comment, and they both leaned in to see what they'd been chasing all this time.

"Is that what I think it is?" he asked as she lifted the injector out of the case and held it up so they could both look at the liquid inside the vial. It was bright silver and flowed like molten metal as she tipped it from side to side.

"It looks just like the medi-bot treatment I injected myself with a few days ago." She checked the injector and then the box it came in. "Yeah. That's what it is. Same batch code as the one I received. I thought the box looked familiar, but I couldn't be sure until I saw it again."

"Son of a starbeast. He was bringing them a sample."

"Why? Don't they already have this technology?"

"They have the original version." He pointed to the injector. "That's something new. And the fastest way to figure out how to counter a new weapon is to steal one and tear it apart to see how it works."

"They could counter it?"

"Maybe. Or use it to improve their own."

She lowered her hand and then stopped and offered it to him. "You should take this."

"No, keep it with you. If anything else happens, you are to take that and run like hell. Then call the *Bat* to come and get you off this rock."

She shook her head and thrust her hand out to him. "No. I mean you should inject yourself with that. Now."

"No." He waved her away. "I'm not taking that."

"Why not? The colonel already offered it to your team. Didn't he?"

"He offered. I'm still considering my options."

She stared at him incredulously. "You almost died a few minutes ago. This whole planet wants to kill us, and we can't let that fall into enemy hands. What's to consider?"

A wall gave way somewhere inside him, and the truth poured through the gap and out of his mouth before he knew what was happening. "I'm dangerous, Bobbi. You've read my file. You know what those scars on my back are from. Right?"

She stood her ground, chin lifted, eyes locked on his. "I know."

"My grandfather was a violent, rage-filled asshole. So was my father. The difference was my father learned to control it. Channel it. So did I."

"The gym. That's why you were there that night." It wasn't a question.

"I'm there every night. It's how I stay in control."

"That's crazy. And it's bullshit. You've been with me

for days and haven't needed to go to the gym to stay in control."

"Because I've been burning it off with you in bed." He caught her by the hips, pulling her to him.

"Yeah?" She grinned up at him, defiant and so sexy it made his blood burn. "So take the damned shot and we can spend every night like that."

"I'm afraid I'll hurt you."

"You won't. But if you accidentally do, I'll heal."

"I'm dangerous."

The little minx laughed at him. Actually threw back her head and laughed. "You say that like it's a revelation." She threw out her arms. "We're in the middle of a jungle on a strange planet. There's a dead body a few meters away, and I'm the one who killed him. You're dangerous. Yes. So is this place." She rose on her toes to kiss him. "And so am I."

"Tell me you aren't afraid of me," he demanded in a voice he barely recognized as his own.

"Again?"

"Say it!"

She stared up at him for a moment, as if trying to read his mind—or his soul. Then she nodded once and touched his cheek. "I'm not afraid of you, and I never will be."

He growled and swung her into his arms. They needed to be doing at least a half-dozen things, but he didn't care about the mission right now. All he could think about, all he wanted, was her.

13

BOBBI'S last coherent thought was to tuck the injector into an empty pouch on her webbing. After that, she stopped thinking at all and just let herself get lost in this moment. Part of her knew she was avoiding facing reality. It was like trying to dance with a Nantari rhino standing in the middle of the room, but she danced anyway.

She carefully nibbled and kissed his neck as he carried her through the brush. He tasted of sweat, earth, and the wipes he'd used to clean the… She stopped that line of thinking before it led her back to a place she wasn't ready to go.

Instead, she focused on him. His strength. His scent. His hazel eyes that reflected the colors of the jungle. Everything about him screamed predator, but that wasn't all he was. She just needed to make him see that. Make him want to take the treatment. If he did, they could stay together and have centuries of life and love and… *whoa*.

She spun away from that thought, too. Forget Nantari rhinos. She was trying to dance in a minefield. The thought made her laugh.

"Something funny?" Kurt asked, his voice still rough and raw from the fight.

"Just my brain. I'm trying not to think too hard and the results are… strange."

"I can help with that." He turned his head to nuzzle her cheek. "We're here. Take a look."

She raised her head and cooed in surprise. She'd been so deep inside her head she hadn't even noticed the changes. The constant chorus of birds and insects had been replaced by the sound of falling water, and the air was full of mist. The waterfall was only a few meters high and spilled into a rocky pool so clear and perfect it was like they'd stepped into a sim-pod program.

"Okay, so, maybe this planet has one redeeming feature."

"Just one, though." He set her back on her feet but didn't let go. Instead, he started unfastening the clips on her webbing. She did the same for him, and within seconds they were tearing at each other's clothes. She needed to see him, to feel him against her, skin to skin. It was more than desire. It was a compulsion.

They shed their gore-stained clothing, cursing and swearing as they had to stop to untie boots and fight to get them off their tired, swollen feet. The second she was barefoot, Kurt tossed her over one shoulder, giving her a fine view of his toned ass as he marched them both into the pool.

"Don't even think about throwing me—asshole!"

she howled as he did exactly what she'd expected and tossed her into the water. It was warm, and as the water closed over her head, she had a moment of perfect peace. Everything went still and quiet, and she let herself sink down until her feet touched the rocky bottom. Then, she opened her eyes, found her target, and launched herself straight at Kurt's legs. He went down hard, and she barely kept herself from laughing until she broke the surface.

"Minx!" he bellowed a few seconds later, rising up from the water like an angry god.

He swept a hand over his face, clearing his vision and pushing his hair back at the same time. When he spotted her, he bared his teeth in a feral smile. "Run."

She squealed and dove back beneath the surface, heading straight for the waterfall. She knew she wouldn't make it that far, but that was the point.

He caught hold of her ankle less than two seconds later, pulling her back through the water until he could wrap her in his arms. "Mine."

His declaration was the most primal, arousing thing any man had said to her. If anyone else had said it, she'd have laughed in their face. But this was Kurt, and that made all the difference.

"Maybe." She kissed him before either of them could say anything else.

His answering kiss was as raw and real as anything she'd ever experienced. She opened her mouth to him and let him take what he needed. What they both craved. Release. Escape. A celebration of their victory and the fact they were still alive.

He walked them under the waterfall. The water beat down on her head and shoulders like another set of hands, massaging aching muscles and washing her clean. When he finally raised his head, she tried to follow him, not wanting the kiss to end. He shook his head sharply and then set her down on a stone ledge. It put them almost eye to eye, but before she could ask why, he gripped her by the hips and spun her around to face the falls. She reached out with both hands, bracing herself against the water as he moved in behind her, one hand on her back, pushing her down as he drew her hips toward him.

She let him guide her, desire curling inside her like a wave ready to break. He arched over her, shielding her from the water. He kissed her shoulder and then bit her in the same spot, sending a spike of heat and need arrowing through her.

His hands found her breasts, teasing and tweaking them, but soon one hand was moving lower over her stomach to the apex of her thighs.

She rose on her toes, anticipation making her pulse quicken and her pussy slick. Still, he didn't say anything. Not that she could have heard him over the water pouring down on them, but she knew he was silent because his mouth pressed to her shoulder and she would have felt the buzz of it against her skin.

He found the seam of her pussy and pushed inside, his fingers quickly becoming coated in her essence. He bit her again, harder this time, and the burn blended with the pleasure as he strummed her clit at the same time.

He plunged a finger inside her and then two, working his fingers in and out in the short, quick strokes he'd learned she liked best. She rode his hand hard, reaching for release, but he withdrew his fingers before she found it.

She looked back over her shoulder, but the angle was wrong and the water hid his face.

He swatted her ass hard enough to sting. She yelped in protest as much as surprise, and he spanked her again.

She raised one hand and flashed him a single digit salute that earned her another light slap, but after that she faced forward and braced both hands against the rocks. As much as she enjoyed sassing him, she wanted him too much to play games right now. She bowed her head and arched her back, giving him what he needed most—her surrender. Her reward came a moment later when he took her in one smooth thrust.

She expected him to take her hard and fast. Instead, he curved one arm around her and then straightened up, drawing her up with him. He placed his free hand next to one of hers on the rocks, his thumb brushing against her fingers in a barely there caress. His lips brushed her ear and then her cheek. She turned her head, their mouths meeting in a hungry kiss.

They moved together in a slow, erotic dance more intense than she could have imagined. Water-slick bodies slid against one another, breath mingled, hips rolling as they came together over and over. He groaned, and she felt his cock begin to thicken and twitch. She flexed her channel around him, pushing him closer to the edge. He moved his hand from her stomach back to her pussy, working her clit with merciless precision.

"Come for me."

His order was barely audible, but that didn't matter to her body. It knew what he wanted and happily obeyed. She came hard, riding his cock and fingers, her cries swept away by the water as soon as they left her lips.

He came with her, emptying himself inside her with sharp jerks of his hips. Her arms gave out, and she had to lean against the rocks for support. He moved with her, a heavy weight against her back as they both panted and shivered through the aftershocks of their lovemaking.

He eased himself away from her a few minutes later, taking her by the hand and helping her out of the falls back into the pool. Neither of them spoke, as if they knew once they did, the spell would be broken and they'd have to return to reality.

Instead, she floated beside him, fingers interlaced, her hand on his shoulder and her head tucked beneath his chin.

After several more stolen moments, she raised her head and moved her hand to touch his throat gently. "Any better?"

"Some. I won't be singing in the shower any time soon, but I'll heal."

"If you took the—" He touched a finger to her lips, stopping her from saying more.

"No."

She wanted to argue. To explain to him all the reasons why it was the right thing to do. It was logical. Tactical. Smart. And he knew every reason she could offer him—even the one she wasn't ready to talk about. If he took the treatment, he'd be like her. Was that part of the reason he was holding back? Because it might tie them together?

She couldn't help but feel like he was rejecting her as well as the nanotech. It was irrational and stupid, but emotions often were. "Okay. I won't bring it up again for at least… twelve hours?"

He smiled a little. "I see your twelve and raise you to twenty-four hours and a hot meal from now."

Her stomach rumbled, reminding her she needed to eat the rest of her lunch. "Deal."

"Food?" he asked.

"Yeah. We need to eat and get going. Don't we?"

"We do." He pointed to their gear. "What say we grab what we need and leave our dirty clothes here? We've both got spare stuff in our packs, and just the thought of putting any of that back on is making my skin itch."

"That sounds like a plan. I'd rather wander through this jungle naked than wear any of that again."

"We won't be naked, though. We'll have boots on. I'll wear my vest and you can wear your webbing."

She snorted. "Very stylish."

He leered and waggled his brows. "I think you're going to look sexy as hell dressed that way."

She raked her gaze over his naked form, which she

could see very well in the clear water of the pool. "So will you."

They moved to the edge slowly and then he lifted her out, pausing to kiss her gently before climbing out as well. Their moment had passed, but she didn't get the sense they were done with each other. Not yet. She went over to her clothes and checked to make sure the injector was still where she'd left it. He might not want to talk about it yet, but that was fine. She needed time to prepare her arguments anyway. He was wrong about who he was, and she was going to prove it.

She wanted him to take the treatment. That thought kept bouncing around Kurt's skull as they dressed and ate. He'd tried to show her who he was and why that wasn't a good idea, but she couldn't see it. Or wouldn't. Or maybe she was right, and he was the one who couldn't see the truth. *Fraxx* if he knew anymore.

Bobbi glowered over at the stand of blackened trees. "I told you this planet was trying to kill us. When it couldn't do it on its own, it sent up a *vething* smoke signal to summon help from our resident bad guy."

"It's just a theory. But how else did he know we were here or where to find us?" They were working their way in ever-expanding circles, looking for Clooney's transport. It had to be somewhere nearby. Bobbi said he'd been clean and tidy when she first saw him, which meant he hadn't walked far.

"It's a good theory. We've been here hours, so it's

unlikely he spotted our arrival. If I hadn't hit those trees, he wouldn't have known we were here."

He pointed to another stand of kaboom trees. "They're everywhere. Honestly, I think we were lucky we got as far as we did before we triggered one. I don't know what's in the sap they're coated in, but it's an arsonist's wet dream. One spark and boom!"

Bobbi made a vague noise of agreement, but her focus was on something to her left.

"See something?"

"Mmm." She took a step to the left and then another. "Found it!"

It was a hover-bike, pristine and gleaming. The charred remains of a tree stood a few meters away. It had happened recently, which explained the hole in the tree canopy. The bike was small enough to drop through the gap.

"The Grays might be evil bastards, but they have some really nice toys," Bobbi said as they walked around the vehicle.

"Advantage of working for the side with all the money," he agreed.

"So they get money, power, fast ships, and the best tech. What's the advantage for being on our side again?"

"Free uniforms, bad food, and the knowledge that we're the good guys."

She snapped her fingers. "Right. I knew there was a reason I signed up."

"Was it the food or the uniforms?"

"The uniforms. But not mine." She bit her lower lip

and uttered a soft little moan that sent a surge of blood and lust straight to his cock. "I'm a sucker for a man in uniform."

"Yeah? As it happens, I've got a closet full of them back home. I will happily model them all for you."

"And I will happily help you out of them afterward." Something in her expression softened for a second. It was so quick even he had trouble interpreting it, but it could have been... hope?

He knew what he was hoping for—more time with her, in uniform or out of it. But to get there, he needed to keep her safe, and so far, he'd done a lousy *fraxxing* job of it. At least her part of the mission was over now. All that was left was to get her and the stolen nanotech back on the *Bat*.

Thunder rumbled in the distance, and both of them looked up warily.

"Guess we better get going before that storm gets any closer. I've had my share of elemental disasters today already," Bobbi said. "Do you know how to fly one of these?"

"I do."

"Good, because the last time I flew a hover-bike I was seventeen years old and there may have been alcohol involved. To say I'm a little rusty would be an understatement."

"So, the daughter of the renowned Justice Castille had a rebellious stage? That's not in your file either."

She smirked. "I admit to nothing. And it's not in my file because I never got caught."

Bobbi stowed their gear while he looked over the

controls. Hover-bikes were common transport on most planets. It had taken a few dozen wrongful death lawsuits to get it done, but the companies that made the bikes had eventually learned to standardize the basic layout so anyone could operate any model anywhere in the galaxy.

He started it up and then patted the seat behind him. "Ready to get out of this jungle?"

"*Fraxx*, yes." She hopped on behind him and then scooted forward until her body was pressed against his back.

"Not wearing the safety harness, then?"

She wrapped her arms around his waist. "Nope. So try not to crash into anything. Besides, there's a shield, right? I'll be perfectly safe."

"Unless I crash, in which case you will bounce around the inside of the shield like popcorn in a bubble."

"Then don't crash. Problem solved."

He sighed, shook his head, and then activated the shield that would protect them both while they were airborne. "Dating you is going to do terrible things to my insurance rates. Isn't it?"

Her laugh rolled through him like the pealing of silver bells. "Possibly. But don't worry. I can afford it."

He was halfway to the treetops before the truth of what she'd said sank in. He knew she came from money and power—generations of it on the Castille side. *Veth*, her family connections were one of the reasons she'd been a suspect in the first place. But her wealth was just another fact he'd learned, like the fact she spent half her vacation time every year working pro bono cases out of her mother Celeste's office and spoke more than a dozen languages and dialects. But that was when she'd been his suspect. Now, she was his everything.

"Son of a *fraxxing* starbeast. I'd forgotten about that. New plan. When we get back to Astek, you are taking *me* out for ice cream."

She squeezed him hard enough his ribs creaked. "It's a date."

They rose above the treetops to a sight so beautiful they both lapsed into silence. The midafternoon sun was lost behind a wall of bruise-dark storm clouds with only a few shafts of deep, golden light streaming through small breaks in the cover. The forest spread out in all directions, a sea of green that shifted and swayed in the rising wind like ripples on a vast pond.

Lightning arced between the towering thunderheads that flowed toward them like a black wall. It was going to be close. He turned the bike away from the storm and toward the base. They were close enough he could see it. It was a geodesic dome of gleaming white surrounded by smaller domes and Clooney's ship.

"Well, that explains how he got to us so fast. I didn't realize we were so close."

"Pity your uncle didn't stash a hover-bike on board. We could have saved ourselves a lot of sweat, blood, and time."

"I'll let him know that the next time we steal his ship, I expect it to be better supplied."

"You go ahead and tell him that." What Kurt needed

to say to Archer would be a lot more cutting and far more likely to earn him a demotion and a transfer to the ass end of nowhere.

He parked the hover-bike on the tarmac near the main building and killed the engine. The first drops of rain pattered on the shield and sizzled as they hit the sunbaked ground.

"Ready?"

She let go of him and sat back. "What's the plan?"

"Grab the gear and then get out of the rain. Overhang by the main doors should work as a staging area."

"Okay."

He didn't mention that was as far as she'd be going. Clooney might be dead, but automated defenses could still be in place. He wouldn't risk her life by taking her in with him.

"Shouldn't we contact Boo and have it bring the *Bat* down?" she asked as they jogged over to the door. The sky was darkening by the second and the rain was coming down harder now.

"Contact the ship, yes. Call it down, no. Not until the storm passes. Ships like that can handle atmospheric flight but not in weather like this." As he gestured around them, a bolt of lightning sizzled across the sky, followed by a clap of thunder so loud it hurt his ears.

"Point taken."

They were both soaked to the skin by the time they reached cover. "We should dry off before we put the rest of our gear on or it's going to chafe."

"I should, yeah."

She froze and then fixed him with a flat stare. "*I.* Not *we*?"

He donned his armored vest before answering, as if that could save him from the wrath that was about to come his way. "You're staying here."

14

Bobbi couldn't believe they were having this conversation again. "The hell I am. I'm going with you."

"No, you're not." Kurt shot her a look that would have warned off a charging Nantari rhino. She ignored it.

"I'm safer with you."

"Not this time."

"Haven't you been paying attention? Leaving me alone is when I get into trouble." She held up a hand, ticking off her points on her fingers. "The fight with the Pheran happened after you left me in the lobby. I spotted Clooney's handoff after you left me by the dancefloor. Both the demon lizard-toad and Clooney came after me while you were doing a walkabout in the woods. What do all those things have in common? You. Weren't. There."

He wrapped a strong hand around hers, closing her fingers. "And in two of your three examples, you ignored my instructions. If you hadn't, you'd have been perfectly safe. So this time, I want you to stay put, don't do anything reckless, and try to avoid pissing off any of the wildlife until I get back."

His touch made her want to melt into his arms, but his words made her want to tear out her hair. "I'm supposed to be with you!" She didn't know if she was talking about the mission or something bigger. Right now, it all felt like the same thing.

"Not this time. I need you to contact Boo and have it send a message to the *Malora*. Give them a sit-rep, tell them what we found, and get an ETA on when they're arriving. I'm trusting you to make sure this door stays open. I have no idea what defenses this place has, and I need to know I've got a secure exit."

She glowered and then pulled her hand out of his grip, her mood suddenly a match for the storm raging around them. "Did you just tell me to guard the door like I'm some low-level character in an RPG? Are there some horses you want me to feed too?"

"I'm going to assume you're not talking about rocket-propelled grenades. Other than that, I have no idea what most of that meant."

"RPG. Role-playing game. Fantasy. Dungeons and—forget it. I'll explain another time."

"Role-play? Are we back to your fondness for men in uniform again?" He managed to keep a straight face for two seconds before he lost the battle to hide his grin.

"Asshole. You *did* know what I meant."

"We've got a running game going on the *Malora*. Three years and counting. Magi taught us all to play."

"And you thought teasing me would distract me from being mad?"

"It did distract you," he pointed out, with only a hint of smugness.

"But I'm still mad."

He moved in close and gathered her into his arms. "I know. I get it. But you're not trained for this. I am. If I thought there was anyone else on this base, I wouldn't be leaving you on your own. I'm just trying to keep you safe."

"Because of my uncle?"

He gently tucked a loose strand of her hair behind her ear, his fingers leaving traces of heat across her skin. The moment he touched her, the world around them faded away. The rain, the storm, even the thunder stopped. Or at least, her awareness of it did.

"Because I want us to go out on a real date someday. Maybe a bunch of dates. Dinner. Dessert. Dancing. Any of it. All of it. That can't happen if something happens to you," he said.

"I'd like that. And that means you need to stay safe too. Especially since you're the stubborn jerk who won't take the damned medi-bot treatment. If I get shot, I'll heal. You won't."

"Then I'll just have to avoid getting shot." He kissed her softly, full lips pressing against hers. His next words were whispered against her mouth. "I like that you're worried about me, though. That's new."

"Well, we haven't known each other that long. All of this is pretty new." *And intoxicating. And terrifying. And oh, so amazing.*

"True. But that's not what I meant. You know I signed up the moment I was old enough. Left my family, the farm." He kept his gaze locked on her as he spoke, and every flash of lightning made the green in his eyes stand out.

"I know. It's all in your file. And now I know why. You thought the military would give you the discipline you needed to control your temper."

"It did."

She was about to argue, to point out he'd done that for himself, but he stopped her with another soft kiss. "Not the point, minx. What I mean is, since I left home, no one has worried about me. I've been on my own. Now…"

She saw hope in his eyes and something far deeper —something that made her want to throw her arms around him and confess to everything. That she loved him. That she was scared for him. That she wanted a lifetime of date nights. Ask why he wouldn't just take the *fraxxing* injection so that could happen. She didn't say any of that, though. If she said part of it, she'd say it all. It wasn't the right time. She'd agreed not to bring it up again until after the mission.

She settled for something less life-altering instead. "Now you've got someone to worry about you. So do me a favor and stay in one piece, please?"

"I'll be back before you know it. And once this storm ends we're going to get on the *Bat*, head for orbit, and do nothing until the others get here."

"And eat ice cream. Naked." She kissed him one last time and then let him go. "Hurry back. And leave your comms on. I'll do the same. At least I'll be able to hear you."

"I will." He paused and touched a hand to her cheek. "Stay safe. If you see anything move out there, *fraxxing* shoot it."

She patted her blaster. "That's the plan."

Bobbi had expected him to spend some time hacking the security system or using some sort of nifty tech to figure out how to outwit the hand scanner at the door. Kurt didn't bother with any of that. He just blasted the security pad until it melted away to slag. Once it cooled off enough to touch, he reached into the wall and tripped the latch by hand. The door slid open and stayed that way.

"Back soon," he said, and then he was gone.

It wasn't ten seconds before she heard blaster fire. A lot of it. She wanted to scream at him and demand to know what was going on, but she bit her lip and stayed silent.

She could hear him swearing and firing, and then… silence. "Kurt?"

"Here. Sorry. I knocked the mic loose, diving for cover. I was right. There are automated defenses in here and they are *not* happy to see me."

"Then get back out here. We can wait until the others arrive to clear the building." They had what they came for. The rest could wait. Couldn't it?

"No can do. I need to find the main system and shut it down before it gets wiped. The Grays don't know we're here yet, but they will soon and once that happens, they'll do what they always do."

She'd read enough of the files to know what that was. "Wipe the system and blow things up for good measure?"

"Yeah."

"And yet, one of us is inside the building and the other is right outside the door. If things go boom, we're going to be nothing but ashes and regret. So again, why are you in there?"

"Because we've still got some time before that happens, and if I can shut down the main system, it won't happen at all."

She was pacing back and forth beneath the overhang now. The air was so hot and humid it was hard to breathe, but she couldn't keep still. Not until she saw him again.

"You stay safe. I'm going to contact the *Bat* now."

She could have spoken to Boo directly, but she didn't want to turn off her link to Kurt, so she typed out her message instead. Where they were, what they'd found, and finished off by asking when the *Malora* would be arriving.

The response was quick, but the answer wasn't what she wanted to hear. Rossi and the rest of the team were still half a day away. Flying after Clooney, she'd willed the *Bat* to pull ahead of the *Malora* to give her a chance to be part of the mission. Now, she couldn't wait for the others to get here.

She rubbed her palms against her pants in slow circles, as if to wipe off the blood she could still feel on her skin. Clooney's blood. If she looked down, she knew her hands would be clean. It didn't matter, though. In her mind, the blood was still there, and part of her was afraid it always would be.

When it got to be too much, she walked out into the rain. Not far enough to be a likely target for the lightning still tearing across the sky, but far enough she could stretch out her arms and let the rain wash her clean. It had been months since she'd been on a planet and experienced actual weather. She threw back her head and twirled, replacing her dark thoughts with memories of jumping in puddles as a little girl. Her mood started to lift, and she laughed as she spun again and spotted someone she didn't know standing in the doorway.

"Humans are so odd," the woman said.

Bobbi drew her blaster and shot her.

That should have been the end of it, but instead of dropping to the ground like the corpse she should have been, the dark-haired woman stared down at the hole in her shoulder with an eerily blank expression.

It wasn't until she raised her head to look at Bobbi again that her features shifted into a look of mild annoyance. "That will be inconvenient."

"Who the *fraxx* are you?" Bobbi demanded, her blaster still trained on the woman. She wore a simple beige shipsuit with no markings or clues as to who she was or where she'd come from.

"I'm Vivian." Her head cocked to one side in an oddly bird-like motion. "And you are not supposed to be here, Lieutenant Commander Castille. Why aren't you on Astek station?"

"How do you know who I am? And why aren't you

dead? I mean, I shot you and you're still standing there. Are you even bleeding?"

Vivian moved impossibly fast, crossing the distance between them so quickly Bobbi didn't realize she'd moved at all until the blaster was knocked out of her hand with enough force to break bones.

She bit back a scream and cradled her broken hand against her body. "Bitch."

"Yes. I've been called that before. Your opinion of me is irrelevant. I need information. Where is Lieutenant Harold Clooney? He should be here."

"*Fraxx* you. You broke my hand. Why would I tell you anything?" It was hard to think through the pain, but she needed to convey as much information to Kurt as she could. Something was niggling at the back of her mind. Something about the name Vivian. She'd come across it before. But where?

"You will tell me because I can hurt you if I have to. Badly. In ways that will leave you begging for your death. Now, where is the lieutenant?"

She looked into the woman's cold, dead eyes and knew she meant every word she'd said. "He's dead."

Vivian stared at her for a long, unblinking moment and then nodded once. "I see. That is also inconvenient. He was delivering a package. It was not inside. Do you have it?"

"You mean the medi-bot treatment he stole from the military? Yeah, that got destroyed in the fight. I guess the IAF didn't think to put that in a blaster-proof package."

"You killed Clooney?"

Bobbi tried not to be insulted by the tone of disbelief in the other woman's voice. She raised her chin and tried to look defiant. "I did."

"Possible, but unlikely. Unless you had help."

Fraxx. She reached for the most plausible lie she could think of… one that wasn't far from the truth. "No help. I'm here alone. There wasn't time to tell anyone else after I saw Clooney make the exchange. Others are coming, but they're not here yet."

"You fought Clooney and have no injuries at all?" Again, Vivian watched her with that unblinking stare that made Bobbi want to fidget.

"You really aren't much for supporting your fellow woman. Are you?" she tossed back.

"I am not for supporting anyone." Vivian's gaze dropped to Bobbi's hand and her brow creased. "Your hand is already healing. How?"

"I wish. It doesn't feel like it from where I'm standing."

"Your physical location is not relevant to my question. I can sense changes in body heat and blood flow that would indicate your body is trying to heal itself. You will explain, or I will damage you in a way that will demonstrate how quickly you heal."

This bitch was really starting to annoy her. "Fine. I was treated with medi-bots before I left."

"Given who you are, it is likely you were given the improved version of the treatment. Excellent. Then the loss of the sample is no longer a problem. You are now my sample."

"Uh, no." Bobbi didn't like the way that sounded. "I'm not going anywhere with you."

She desperately hoped that whatever Kurt was planning, he did it soon. Whoever or whatever Vivian was, she had no interest in becoming part of her plans.

～

Once he learned where the building's automated defenses were positioned, Kurt's exploration started to feel like a training exercise. Enter a new section. Identify targets. Remove targets. Move forward. Repeat.

He could hear Bobbi though his earpiece. A tread of her boot, the occasional sigh, the rumble of thunder and the hiss of falling rain. It was comforting to know she was out there, bored but safe, while he secured the building.

There wasn't much to secure. The dome was large, but from what he could tell the entire center was a single room. By the time he got to it, though, he felt like a rat in a maze. He couldn't decide if the layout was the result of a drunk designer or an elaborate security measure, but it took him longer than he would have liked to reach the inner core.

He had to blast another palm scanner to get through the last door, but once he stepped inside, he immediately knew that nothing about the design of this place could be an accident.

The inner room was indeed a large, circular room that rose all the way up to the domed ceiling. That was all he got right, though.

He'd imagined a lab of some sort, some mad scientist's lair just waiting for a legion of white-coated lab monkeys to arrive and whip up the Gray Men's next evil plan. It turned out their plan was already in progress.

The taupe-colored walls were lined with cryo-pods, though only the ones on the main floor were in use. Rows of green lights glowed on the displays of half a dozen pods. Plush recovery couches were set into the walls, along with dispensers that sat waiting to offer food and drink to the newly revived. The place looked more like medical spa than a laboratory.

He heard Bobbi laughing over the open line, the sound of splashing accompanying it. At least one of them was having fun.

He was about to tell her to come inside and see what he'd found when he heard someone else speak. Followed by the sound of a blaster.

He spun around to race back to Bobbi and finally saw the other two pods. They were set into the wall on either side of the door. Both were empty, but one still had traces of frost on the door, and its blinking lights indicated it had recently brought its inhabitant out of cryo-sleep.

He broke into a dead run. Another of the Grays was awake... and they'd found Bobbi. If they lived through this, he swore by all the stars in all the galaxies he would never leave Bobbi alone again.

Listening to what happened next was the hardest thing he'd ever done because there was nothing he could do to stop it. He was too far away. He'd figured out enough of the layout to take some shortcuts on the way back, but it wasn't enough. As he ran he heard everything that happened outside. Bobbi's pain, her fear, and her brilliant way of conveying as much information as she could to him without tipping off the other woman. Vivian.

The name alone was enough to conjure up a sense of dread. They didn't know much about her, other than she worked with Dr. Absalom, the sociopathic scientist who had created the rogue AI V.I.D.A and invented the technology that spawned the cyborgs. They'd crossed paths with her twice—once going after Absalom and again when they'd been part of a hostage retrieval mission.

Her body was a clone of a dead woman, an agent of the Gray Men who had been tasked with controlling a pair of cyborg assassins. She went by a different name now, and no one knew anything about this version. She was a dangerous mystery, one he needed to take down. Fast.

Part of him wanted to run straight back to Bobbi, but he knew that wasn't the smart play. Instead, he turned down a side corridor and hoped it led him to another door, one out of sight of Bobbi and her captor. If he ran into them inside, Bobbi would be between him and his target, and there were too many ways that could go wrong. He had to find another way to reach her.

He was running so fast he nearly missed the door. It blended into the wall with only a simple release bar running across the center. When he hit the bar, it opened outward instead of sliding back and he stumbled out into the rain.

Two of the outbuildings directly ahead of him acted as landmarks, showing him exactly where he was. He turned to the right and jogged around the edge of the dome, not daring to go faster in case the noise gave him away.

"Uh, no. I'm not going anywhere with you," Bobbi was talking to Vivian, but he was so close now he could hear her voice without the radio.

He crept forward now, hoping like hell he'd have a clean shot at Vivian when she came into sight. He'd heard Bobbi say she'd shot the woman once already, but it hadn't had much effect. Was she shielded? Wearing body armor?

Bobbi came into sight first. Her arm was close to her body, skin pale, and lips pressed together in a grimace of pain and pure determination. She was soaked to the skin, the rain plastering her clothes and hair to her body. If she saw him, she gave no sign. Her focus was all on someone still out of sight.

"I don't need you alive." The other voice sounded bored, as if she were having a tiresome conversation with a stubborn child. "So you might want to reconsider your resistance. Either you come with me willingly and I let you live, or you say no one more time and I kill you and take what I need. The second option is simpler for me. So choose wisely."

That certainly sounded like the bitch the others had described. Cold. Dispassionate. Ruthless. *Dangerous*. He readied himself, raised his blaster, and moved until he could see his target. Then he opened fire.

He hit her twice in rapid succession, once in the chest and a second strike in almost the same place as Bobbi's shot. The bitch didn't so much as stumble as she broke into a run and came at him at impossible speed.

Not human. The thought flew through his brain as he fired another shot, catching her in the face this time.

The skin melted away along with part of her cheek, leaving a pitted hole that leaked milky fluid instead of blood.

"What the *fraxx*?" It was all he had time to say before she hit him hard enough to send him flying backward.

They hit the ground hard, both of them lashing out with hands and feet, trying to inflict damage on the other. He quickly realized that while she was far stronger than he was, she wasn't a trained fighter. She relied on brute force to get the job done, and that might save him. It had to because if he went down, Bobbi would die too.

They rolled across the tarmac, his ribs screaming in protest at this new abuse. He was going to be in trouble if this fight went on too long. He had one chance to win, and it meant doing the one thing he swore he'd never do. He reached down into the darkest part of his soul and unleashed a lifetime's worth of pain and rage, directing it all at the creature that threatened the woman he loved.

15

BOBBI WATCHED in horror as the two tore at each other. They snarled and fought like animals, grunts of pain and anger filling the air. She ran to get her blaster, which was half submerged in a puddle of rainwater some distance away. Vivian's blow had sent it much farther than she would have thought possible, which explained her shattered hand. Whatever the hell Vivian was, she was not entirely human.

She hissed in pain as she bent over to grab the weapon. It was wet and slippery and she was one-handed at the moment, but eventually she slammed it against her thigh and managed to get a proper hold. Then she turned and ran straight to Kurt.

He had Vivian down on the ground, using his blaster as a club. The noise was sickening, but the only blood she saw was running down a cut across Kurt's nose. Vivian was leaking something white and viscous, and when Bobbi got closer, she saw there was nothing human about the thing Kurt was fighting. It was a synthetic—an abomination so unthinkable that when laws had been drafted to prevent their creation, many dismissed the idea as a sign the Unified Galactic Courts were afraid of boogeymen. They weren't supposed to be possible, but she was looking at one.

One of her arms lay inert across the ground, but she was using the other to block Kurt's blows. It was clear that Kurt was tiring quickly, but once she was a little closer, she'd be able to help. They'd take the thing down together.

Twenty strides. Fifteen. Ten. She raised her blaster and trained it on the thing's mangled head. "Sabre, get clear!"

He threw himself back, raising his hands to give her a clear shot. The move left him open, though, and at the same moment Bobbi fired, Vivian slammed her good hand into the soft tissues of his stomach so hard he was thrown into the air and landed in an unmoving sprawl near the thing's feet.

"Kurt!" Her scream was drowned out by a distant boom of thunder. She wanted to go to him, to find out how badly he was hurt, but she needed to deal with the threat first.

There wasn't much left of the thing that had called itself Vivian. Her shot had blasted away part of her throat, destroying whatever passed for her spinal cord in the process. Vivian stared up with her one still-working eye, the expression as cold and dead as ever.

Doubt made her hesitate for a moment. Did she put this thing down now, or leave her in hopes that she might survive until the *Malora* got here and they could interrogate her? "V-v-very. Incon-con-con-venient," she stammered suddenly and Bobbi nearly blasted it out of instinct.

"Yeah, you are."

Vivian blinked and moved its eye so she could see her. "You-ou think you have w-wo-won?"

Bobbi moved to stand between the thing and Kurt, blaster still leveled at her head. "Pretty sure we did." So long as Kurt was alright. But she couldn't check until she dealt with this thing.

"You-ou did not. T-ell Magi I will ave-ave-avenge my twin." The word ended with an exhaled breath, and there was no following inhalation. Her ruined mouth twitched into an obscene, lopsided smile, and the light went out of her eye. Click. Gone. Like someone had flicked a switch.

"Not creepy at all. Nope," she muttered and blasted her in the face for good measure. If she was down, she wanted her to stay that way. She holstered her blaster and hurried over to Kurt.

He was on his back, both hands folded over a spot on his left side. His jaw was clenched and he was taking short, shallow breaths that hissed through his teeth. His lips were pale and flecked with blood, though she couldn't tell if that was from an injury to his mouth or something far more serious.

"I hate to say I told you so…" she said as she dropped to her knees beside him, her broken hand protesting the sudden movement. "But I *fraxxing* told you not to leave me alone. Every time you do, you have to come back and save me, and then I have to save you."

He managed a small grin. "Lesson learned. Won't happen again."

"It better not. Clearly I cannot be trusted on my own." She tried to keep her tone light, but it was a losing battle. He was hurt. "How bad is it? The storm is clearing, I can have the *Bat* come down and we'll get you on board."

She had no idea how she'd manage to get him onto the ship without doing more damage, but there had to be a way. She had her comms out of her pocket and was about to call for help when Kurt shook his head.

"No time." It might have been her imagination, but his voice seemed weaker now.

"I'll tell Boo to hurry. There's a doc-in-a-box on board. It'll fix you right up. And you've already got a dose of healing accelerant in your system. You're going to be fine."

She set the comm unit down on his chest and seized his wrist. Her next words came out tight with fear. "Do you hear me, Sabre?"

"I'm dying, not deaf."

"No. Don't you dare say that."

He raised a hand to cover hers. "She busted up my insides with that last punch. Broke my ribs, too." He winced. "That smarts."

"I'll get the first aid kit. There are pain-blockers. We can…"

He shook his head again. "Don't go."

She had tears in her eyes, and the laugh that tore out

of her chest was thick with grief and fear. She couldn't lose him. Not now. "Isn't that my line?"

"I'm borrowing it."

She scooted closer and got herself seated cross-legged. It took a few careful moves and it hurt like hell, but she managed to get his head cradled in her lap.

"What can I do?" she asked, still holding his hand. She was crying openly now.

"You're doing it. Stay with me."

Anger flared hot, cutting through her grief. "I'm not the one who's leaving. You said you learned your lesson, dammit. That means you can't go."

"I don't want to." He squeezed her hand. "I still haven't taken you out for ice cream."

"You haven't. You've got promises to keep. Don't you dare break them."

She knew there had to be something she could do. Some way to fix this, but her brain wasn't working anymore. All she could think about was Kurt. She'd seen too much death already. Losing him might be more than she could take.

"Tell me you're not afraid of me. After what I did to her."

She stared at him. "You're still worried about that? Now? You kicked a synthetic's ass and saved mine in the process. There is nothing in the galaxy that would make me afraid of you." She sucked in a breath and then added. "I'm not afraid of you. I'm afraid of living the rest of my very long life without you."

Her very long life. Her unnaturally long... *Fraxx*. The pieces finally clicked into place. "I'm an idiot, and you're not dying today." She pulled her hand free of his and fumbled at the pouch near her waist. The one she'd tucked the injector into.

"Medi-bots!" she announced a few seconds later and then glowered down at him. "And don't you even try to tell me no this time. This is happening."

"And you say I'm the bossy one." He eyed the injector with resignation and something that might have been relief. "I forgot about that stuff."

"So did I. Which makes us both idiots."

She checked the injector and then leaned over him. "And for the record, you are absolutely the bossy one. And I love you anyway." She pressed it to the side of his neck and injected him with the medi-bot treatment.

Cold fingers encircled her wrist, and he managed a grin that made her heart soar despite her fear. "Yeah? Good to know. As it happens, I love you too."

She dashed away her tears with the back of her hand and smiled down at him, using her body to protect him from the last of the rain. She had no idea if the nanotech would be enough to save him, so she stayed where she was, counting every breath he took.

They talked in whispered snatches of conversation, never letting the silence go on too long. She held his hand and stroked his cheek by turns, doing everything she could to hold on to him and keep him with her.

By the time the sun came out, she thought his color looked better. As steam started to rise from the tarmac, she was certain his breathing was improving. Her clothes were almost dry before she was certain he was going to be okay.

"Hey, Lieutenant Commander Bossyboots. You can sleep now."

He hummed softly in agreement, his eyes already closed. He looked like crap, but he was going to live. She was sure of it. She cried again, tears of relief this time. She was glad no one could see her right now. All these tears would be hell on her reputation.

She contacted Boo and told the AI to bring down the ship. Kurt might be on the mend, but he'd heal faster once she could get him onto the *Bat* and have the onboard medical system treat him. She couldn't wait to get the hell off this planet.

Whatever he'd found inside could wait. She was starting to come around to his way of thinking. Her mission was over and she wasn't sure she wanted to do another one. Ever.

16

HE HAD the mother of all hangovers and no recollection of the last few hours of consciousness. That hadn't happened since he'd been a much younger, dumber version of himself.

"What the hell did I do last night," he muttered, grimacing as his words came out in a raspy growl. His tongue felt like it was wrapped in dry cotton, and the sunlight streaming through the window was unpleasantly bright.

His brain stuttered. Sunlight? No. He'd been on a station. Or a ship? He cracked open one eye, trying to figure out where the *fraxx* he was and regretted it immediately. "Too bright. Computer dim lights and give me a status report."

He heard a snort of amusement from somewhere to his left. "Your status is beat to shit and lucky to be alive."

"Blink?" He turned toward the sound and opened his eyes again. Lieutenant Aria Jessop was lounging in a chair not far away, a blade dancing between her fingers as she grinned at him. "Welcome back, sir."

Memories came flooding back. Jungle. Fighting. Waterfalls and… "How long was I out? Where am I? Where's Bobbi?"

"You've been out the better part of a day. You're on the *Bat*, which is now docked in the shuttle bay of the Malora. You would not believe the trouble we had to go through to make enough room for this little beauty." The knife vanished back into its arm sheath, and she reached out to pat the nearest bulkhead. "Do we have to give her back?"

"I promised Archer his ship and his niece were coming back in one piece, so, yeah. And you haven't answered my question. Where is Bobbi?" He had to squirm out sideways to escape the claustrophobic confines of the doc-in-a-box.

"She's sleeping. Finally. Wouldn't leave your side until Trip swore on his mother's grave that you'd pull through."

"Trip's mother is alive, though. Clothes?"

"Not for lack of wishing it otherwise, but yeah, she is. It got the point across to your little JAG officer, though. Medi-bots or not, she was exhausted. She even made Fido come over here to debrief her because she didn't want to let you out of her sight. She's quite something." Aria reached down and grabbed a bag from beside her chair and then tossed it to him.

It was one of his, and inside he found fresh clothes from his own closet. "Thanks."

"Bobbi is very special," he agreed as he dressed. "But I'm not sure she's a JAG officer anymore."

"No?" Aria raised a dark brow. "What else could she be?"

"One of us." He still didn't love the idea, but if that's what she wanted, he wasn't going to stand in her way. Bobbi had more than proven herself capable.

"And you'd be okay with that?"

He caught the weight behind the question. Even with his brain still in neutral, he recognized the need to choose his next words carefully.

"Water?"

She tossed him a bottle. Chilled. Hell yes.

He popped the cap and took several long swallows before answering. "A couple of weeks ago my answer would have be no. But I talked to our fearless leader about this before I left, and then Bobbi and I wound up partners for this last mission. Now? I realize Fido is smarter than he looks. He told me the best way to protect her was to train her well and trust her to do the job."

Aria wound a finger around a tightly curled lock of her hair. "That's it? What about team dynamics? Perceived favoritism? Pardon my Pheran, but what about not shitting where we eat?"

"I think that ship has left orbit already. We've got two couples on this team already, and so far, they haven't caused any real problems."

"So far," Aria didn't sound convinced. "And you're forgetting about rank. Bobbi holds the same one you do."

"Oh, that's easy. She's already agreed that I'm the bossy one, so I'm taking that to mean she understands I'm the one in charge."

Aria's dark eyes went wide and she looked at him like he'd lost his mind. It wasn't a look he was used to getting from his teammates. "Uh huh. Sure. Bobbi, want to weigh in here and let my XO know just how wrong he is?"

"He's adorably deluded."

Kurt spun around just in time to catch Bobbi as she flew into his arms, though she was careful not to squeeze him too hard. Her eyes shone with unshed tears and she was looking at him like the universe had given her everything she'd ever asked for all at once. No one had ever looked at him like that before. It was the best feeling in the galaxy.

"You're awake. You're awake and you're standing and you're... wait." She leaned back and glowered, an expression he found more adorable than intimidating. "Why are you up? And dressed? No, no, no. You nearly died. Get your ass back in that bed. Or a chair." She pointed to Aria. "You, up! Why is he on his feet?"

Aria threw up her hands and got to her feet. Standing, she was half a head taller than Bobbi. "Cool your boosters, Jaguar. He's fine. Look at him. And I wasn't going to let him leave the ship."

"You weren't? Don't I need to debrief? Talk to the team?" he asked Aria and then looked down at Bobbi. "I'm fine. I'm not going back to bed. How's your arm?" *Veth*, he really needed a coffee if he was going to be required to hold two conversations at once.

Aria folded her arms across her chest. "Nope. You're staying here. Bobbi's right, you nearly died, which means you've earned a rare day off. Enjoy it."

"But the mission."

Bobbi grumbled and tugged at his shirt. "Hey! Your girlfriend, who is in better shape than you are right now, would like to kiss you and tell you how happy she is you're alive. *Fraxx* the mission."

"Girlfriend, huh?" He liked the way that sounded.

"You said you loved me. Thus, I am your girlfriend."

Aria groaned. "Oh no. Not you too?"

"I don't remember that." It was a lie, of course. He remembered it all now. The fight with Vivian. His fear for Bobbi. Her tears. The regrets when he thought they were out of time. The relief when she'd remembered the medi-bots. The way she'd stayed with him.

"Liar." She rose on her toes to kiss him. He picked her up, ignoring the warning twinges from his still-healing torso, to kiss her properly. For a moment as he lay on the tarmac, he thought they'd done this for the last time. He'd never been so grateful to be wrong.

"You're supposed to be taking it easy," Bobbi reminded him when he came up for breath.

"Maybe I need you to take me to bed and make sure I do that?"

Aria clapped her hands over her ears. "Ugh. You two are excessively cute and I'm about to be sick. Please tell me this crap is not contagious."

Bobbi reached over and rubbed her hand over Aria's

shoulder. "Totally contagious. Now you have love cooties too."

"'And now I have to decontaminate." Aria gave a mock shudder and then waved. "Sabre, Jaguar, your asses stay on this ship or I'll call in Buttercup to babysit. And I mean that literally. Dante volunteered to sit on you if you don't stay put. Rest. You earned it. Both of you." She was gone ten seconds later.

"Jaguar?" he asked once they were alone.

"Apparently Magi decided I needed a nickname. I had no say in the creative process."

"Yeah. He does that. But only with people he likes."

"Well, I did save the life of his team's XO, so…" Despite her jokes and laughter, he could see she was tired. The bone-weary kind that not even cutting-edge nanotech could counter.

"You did. And I'm here." He folded her deeper into his arms and held on until he felt her tension ease. She uttered a deep, soulful sigh and melted against him.

"Sorry."

"Why? Because you were worried about me? Because you care?"

"I was going to apologize for being all weepy and emotional, but I like your version better."

He kissed the top of her head. "If we start doing apologies, we're going to be here awhile. I owe you half a dozen or so."

"This is true."

"The thing is, I'm hungry. And I need a shower. So, maybe we can hold off on those for a bit?"

"If there's a shower on offer? I'm good with

postponing any and all apologies."

"Deal. And while we're scrubbing an entire ecosystem out of our hair, you can catch me up on everything that happened while I was out, starting with what that thing said to you before you terminated her."

Bobbi went quiet. "I didn't, though. Not exactly. In fact, Magi and the others don't think Vivian's actually dead."

Dread wrapped its icy talons around his guts and squeezed. "What do you mean it's not dead? You destroyed it. I heard you."

"I destroyed that body, yes. But the thing inside it? Vivian? That was gone before I took my last shot. Magi thinks she escaped into the data sphere the same way Absalom did."

"So Vivian isn't just a synthetic construct. She's someone's digitized consciousness." What he'd seen inside the cryo-lab took on a new, more sinister aspect. "That's what all this is. A digital uploading center. A hub. For *people*." The idea left him nauseated. All those cryo-pods sitting empty. Waiting.

"People. Plural? There were more in there?"

"Yeah. Six. I need to talk to Rossi right away." So much for his day off. He needed to tell the others what he'd seen, and what it meant. He thought they were stashing people away to hide them from detection, or maybe to prepare for some new phase of their plan, but it was so much worse than that. They were gathering an army and sending them into cyberspace. That's what Clooney had been raving about. Immortality. It all made sense now.

Bobbi sat next to Kurt in the *Malora's* briefing room, listening to everything that was said and trying to organize it all into one cohesive whole. Even with her previous security briefings and access to all of their files, there were names she didn't recognize and situations she hadn't retained the details about. She was doing her best to fill in the gaps. She was also amazed and over-the-moon happy to have Kurt at her side. She'd been terrified she would lose him. Even after she'd been banished to the bedroom to sleep, her dreams had been filled with nightmares where the medi-bots failed to work. Worse were the ones where Kurt had lived but blamed her for *infecting* him. Part of her was still afraid that might happen, but she couldn't dwell on it right now. They had work to do.

It was one thing to know that Kurt's team were good at their job and quite another to witness it firsthand. Information flowed from everyone present, adding to their collective understanding and quickly building a picture that was clear, detailed, and more than a little terrifying.

The Gray Men had never been concerned with obeying the law. They believed they were above the restrictions that governed this part of the galaxy. But this... What they were doing wasn't merely breaking the laws. They were shattering them.

"Did you see their faces? Any of them? Do we know who we're going to find down there?" Aria asked.

"I didn't. Their faces were obscured and there were

no ID tags on the pods. Nothing about who was inside. At least, not that I saw. I wasn't there long. Vivian attacked Bobbi right after I got to the core. We must have just missed each other in the halls." Kurt glanced over to her and gave her hand a squeeze beneath the table. "I wish I'd found her first."

"I don't. I shot her and she busted my hand. If you'd done it, she might have killed you, and there was no way I could have done what you did."

Magi grinned. "Yeah, you took down at a *fraxxing* synth, Sabre. You are going to be a legend when we get back."

"Sorry to interrupt, but do we know if there's anything to go back to? Have we heard from anyone?" Bobbi asked.

Trinity looked guilty. "Sorry. I should have mentioned it at the start of this meeting. We heard from Colonel Bahl a few minutes before Sabre called us together. Astek is still there. It's a bit of a mess apparently, but nothing that can't be fixed. She's redirecting Team Four to assist in our investigation, and Archer insisted on coming along. They're on their way to meet us."

Bobbi leaned back in her chair, relief coursing through her. Uncle Scott was alive. She'd been afraid he was gone. That the Grays had managed to take someone else from her. "Thank you. That's good to hear."

"My bad. I should have let you know sooner. Family is important. It's just still weird to think of Archer as *having* a family."

Everyone around the table laughed, including her.

Dax waited until the laughter died away before bringing everyone back to task. "Magi, do you have any idea who Vivian was referring to when she said you killed her twin?"

The cyber-jockey raised his hands. "No *fraxxing* clue. It's not like I've killed a lot of people. I checked and none of them were twins."

"She was glitching and stuttering by that point, but I'm sure that's what she said. And she called you Magi."

"Ex-girlfriend?" Aria suggested, grinning.

"Better not be," Nyx muttered.

"Nope. I can safely swear I have never been involved with twins outside my imagination," Eric said.

Everyone around the table groaned.

Eric leaned forward. The smile was gone from his face. "There is one other possibility, though."

Everyone stilled. Bobbi felt the shift in energy. There'd been an underlying tension in the room, and now it was coming to the surface.

Dax nodded. "Say it. I think we're all thinking it."

"We know Absalom made a copy of V.I.D.A and it's still out there. What if Vivian isn't a digitized consciousness? What if she's always been digital, and now that crazy bastard has given her a body?" Eric asked.

His words had the unmistakable ring of truth to them. He was right. That thing she'd met down on the surface had never been human. It explained a few things, like the strange disconnect between Vivian's words and her expressions as well as her cold, flat gaze. Vivian was a soulless construct. The idea was horrifying.

"Do we think she's got more bodies she can download into?" she asked.

Cris looked at her, and she saw her feelings mirrored in his eyes. "*Fraxx*. I hope not."

"We have to assume that's a possibility." Dax rapped his knuckles on the table. "Which means we need to go down there and secure the base as quickly as possible. We can't wait for Archer and the other Nova Force team to get here."

"Commander Allen will be pissed if we don't wait for her and her team," Dante stated, his expression making it clear he wasn't worried about it.

"She'd make the same call if our positions were reversed. With the info Kurt gave us and what we know about Vivian, I'm making the call. We're going down there."

He looked over at Aria. "You've got the *Malora* doing constant scans. Any sign of activity?"

"Nothing. No life signs bigger than one of Bobbi's demon toads. But that makes sense because cryo-pods lower their occupant's life-signs to the point they'd be undetectable. We had no way of knowing."

"And we didn't want to send out a drone in case it triggered any of the system's defenses, like those fraxxing self-destructs these assholes are so fond of. That shouldn't be a problem now we know they've got people in there," Dante said.

"We can't assume that," Dax said.

"Surely they wouldn't to kill their own people," Cris said and then sighed. "I take that back. This is the Grays we're talking about. They might."

"Exactly. So we go in carefully. Assume everything is a trap. Get what we can and get out again in one piece." Dax pointed to Kurt and then at Bobbi. "And when I say we, I do *not* mean you two. You're sitting this one out."

Kurt grumbled. "I'm fine."

Cris snorted. "As your medic, I'm sorry to tell you that you are not even close to fine. You need time and rest."

Bobbi sat quietly, trying to figure out how she felt about being left behind. Not long ago she would have been angry and disappointed, doing everything she could to change the commander's mind. She didn't feel that way now. She wasn't upset at all. In fact, all she felt was relief.

"Do you really want to go back down there, Kurt? The heat? The humidity? Demon toads?" she asked.

Kurt looked at her in surprise. "You're good with staying here?"

"I am." The answer brought her a surprising amount of peace.

"Then I'm staying, too. I've learned my lesson. There's no way I'm letting you out of my sight again, minx. Stars know what might happen if I do. Space pirates, maybe, or an army of those demon toads, or ship-eating wormholes."

Dax looked at them with amusement. "So glad you agree with my order. Alright, people, let's move. Magi, I want drones inside that building as soon as possible so we know what we're dealing with. Buttercup, get the *Malora* down there, but make sure to park her a nice, safe distance away. Blink and Trip, figure out what equipment you'll need to assess the medical status and identity of our frozen friends. Trinity, you're leading this merry band."

"I am?"

"You are. I can coordinate from here."

The team all looked at each other, grinning.

"Whoohoo! Field trip with no adult supervision!" Eric whooped.

"Hey! I'm an adult," Trinity protested.

"Yeah, but you're more like the cool aunt who lets us eat pizza past our bedtime. This is going to be fun!" Magi left the room with Nyx following after him, her expression somewhere between amused and annoyed.

Dax looked at Kurt and laughed. "I guess that makes us the stodgy parents?"

Kurt leaned back in his chair. "I'm good with that."

Bobbi just sat quietly and smiled to herself. She understood now. All this time, she thought she wanted to be part of the fight. That wasn't it, though. She wanted to be part of a team. She glanced down at their joined hands and then around the room at the rest of Kurt's team.

She had that now. She just needed to figure out a way to keep it.

17

It was strange to be sitting in the *Malora's* climate-controlled briefing room and listen to the chatter of the rest of the team as they bitched about the heat outside. They were almost to the main building now, weapons hot and ready for action despite their casual banter. Feeds from each of their suits appeared on the room's main screen, along with the view from the ship's main camera.

She was almost as tense as they were, and she kept catching herself trying to lean forward, as if she could see more that way.

"Not easy. Is it?" Kurt asked. He was sitting beside her, his fingers drumming the tabletop.

"No. I thought it would be. But this is…" She waved a hand at the screen. "It's frustrating."

"I hate it," Dax's voice came in over the speaker. He was on a ship's channel the others couldn't hear.

"So why aren't you out there?" she asked. Dax was

in the cockpit, ready to take off in a hurry of things went to hell.

"Because if he was, someone else would have to stay behind. Dante gets stuck flying the ship on a lot of missions. Trin runs comms most of the time."

"So it's their turn?" she asked Kurt.

"Exactly. Also, it's insanely hot out there and I'm not a fan of bugs. This way, everyone wins," Dax said.

The three of them lapsed into silence as Trinity and the others approached what was left of Vivian. Their cameras all showed the same grim view, and Bobbi shifted in her chair as dark memories rushed in.

Kurt tugged at her hand. "Come here."

She let him draw her out of her chair and onto his lap. It was the first chance they'd had to be alone for more than a few minutes since he'd woken up, and she felt oddly shy as she curled up in his arms. "Hi."

"Hey." He kissed her softly, distracting her from the screen. "You okay?"

"Mostly." She raised the hand Vivian had broken. Cris had treated it last night, making sure it all healed cleanly. "Does it ever come off?"

Kurt frowned. "Does what... Oh." He captured her fingers gently in his. "I wish I could tell you it does. But the answer is more complicated than that. The lives we take stay with us, but I always figured that was a good thing. It means we're still human."

He kissed her fingers and then nodded toward the screen. "But Vivian was never human. You can't kill something that was never alive to begin with."

"Clooney was."

"Clooney made his choice a long time ago. His death was of his own making, not yours."

"That's a very rational argument. Does it help?"

"Sometimes. And I'll be here to remind you every day you need to hear it."

"Is that what you want?" The question had been lurking in the back of her mind since she'd known for certain he would live. Everything they'd said had been in the heat of the moment, both of them pushed past their limits by pain and circumstance. Had he meant it? Or was he having regrets now?

"Is this your way of giving me an out?" Kurt asked, his voice soft. "Because I don't need it. I meant everything I said. I love you. You're fascinating, smart, stubborn, and sexy. Not to mention you clearly need someone to temper your reckless side."

Joy bubbled up inside her. She'd needed to hear him say it. To make it real. "And you need someone to watch your back."

"Clearly. So, yes, I want this. You. Us. All of it." He tangled his hand in her hair and pulled her in for a slow, hungry kiss that banished every doubt she had left. His mouth moved against hers in a sensual caress that made her forget where they were and that there was anything else in the universe other than the two of them.

"I want all of it, too. You. The team. Everything."

"Training you might just kill me, but we'll make it work."

"Training me?" She stopped and pulled back from him. "No. No training. Well, maybe some. My self-defense moves could use some work, but I don't want to join the team. I just want to belong to it."

"That... But... Uh." He frowned. "You can't be on the team if you're not trained for it."

An idea was taking shape in her mind. "I think maybe I can."

"I hate to interrupt this touching moment, but you two might want to put a pin in your conversation and take a look at the screen. They're about to enter the core."

"*Fraxx*. You heard that? Sorry, Commander."

"Don't be. It's nice to know someone on this team actually listens to my advice."

She gave Kurt a sidelong glance. "Advice?"

"Hush. They're going in," Kurt deflected.

She let him. Later, she'd want details.

Dante went in first, and she focused on his feed. She saw the pods Kurt had described. As Dante turned she saw all six active pods and the two empties—one of which had clearly been Vivian's. They'd decided the other must have been for Clooney. They'd promised him immortality, but what she saw on the screens looked more like a nightmare to her. Frozen bodies. Living minds reduced to data and left to roam the data spheres untethered from reality or any kind of life.

"Holy *fraxx*. Look at this place." Dante directed his camera upward, recording the tiers of empty cryo-pods. Row after row, floor after floor.

"I'm going to have nightmares for weeks," Aria said.

Cris uttered a low whistle. "I don't believe it. We'll

need DNA to confirm, but I think this is Dr. Absalom! The original version."

Everyone spun to look at the pod Cris was pointing to. "Right face. Right age."

"Well, guess we're safe enough. No way they'd blow up their favorite mad scientist," Dante said.

"Stay focused. Keep going. Magi, get what you can out of the computer. Nyx, watch his back while he's inside the system. Aria, give Trip a hand getting readings on the active pods. Buttercup, try to get as much footage as you can of the other levels and the pods." Trinity's orders got them all moving.

"That's my girl," Dax said proudly, but it was on the ship channel so no one outside could hear him.

The team worked fast and efficiently, calling out updates and checking in with Trinity every few minutes. It was almost impossible to tell they were on edge, but she could hear it in their breathing and the brittle edge to their words whenever they spoke.

"How much longer?" she asked in a whisper. She could have sworn they'd been inside for an hour by now.

"It's only been ten minutes. They need at least twice that to get everything we're hoping for," Kurt answered in a normal voice that felt far too loud until she remembered the team couldn't hear them right now.

"Sitrep, Trin. How much longer?" Dax asked over the team's channel.

It made her feel better to know she wasn't the only one who wanted them out of there.

"Fifteen to twenty minutes. Miss me already?" Trinity asked.

"Always, Butterfly," Dax replied.

"That's sweet," Bobbi murmured.

Kurt didn't answer. He was staring at the feeds. He reached out and tapped a button on the comm device on the table in front of them. "Nyx. Turn to your left. More. More. Stop."

"What am I looking at?" Nyx asked a second later.

"*Fraxx*. I don't know, but it wasn't flashing red the last time you panned by. Get Magi out of the system. Now! Trinity, haul ass. My gut is telling me you're out of time."

"Move it!" Dax yelled. "Go. Go. Go!"

To Bobbi, the next few seconds looked like pure chaos. Feeds jumped and spun as the team turned and hauled ass, taking what equipment they could with them as they ran.

"*Fraxx* you, bitch! I got it," Eric yelled and it took her a second to realize he wasn't speaking to anyone on his team.

"Damn it, Magi, move!" Aria yelled.

"I've got him," Nyx shouted back.

"Magi stayed to grab more data. Chaos has him now. I'm bringing up the rear. Still no alarms or any sign of trouble," Aria reported.

Nyx and Magi's feeds were a blur as the cyborg raced through the corridors to catch up to the others.

Kurt and Bobbi watched in silence, hands locked together as they waited, hoping that whatever might be about to happen didn't start until everyone was out of danger.

Magi's feed steadied, the *Malora's* camera showing him standing some distance from the dome now. Nyx was gone again, reappearing a few seconds later with one arm locked around a startled looking Cris.

She went back again to retrieve Trinity and then Dante, manhandling the big part-Torski male like he was a featherweight instead of two meters of solid muscle. Then, the cyborg had gone back in after Aria.

"Come on," Bobbi urged the screen, waiting for Nyx to reappear again. "Where are they?"

"Any sec—" The explosion was deafening, the sound coming in on every feed at once. The ground shook, the ship groaned and shifted, and everyone outside hit the tarmac.

The feeds jumped and sputtered, some flaring white and others going black. For several long seconds, the Malora's view was nothing but static. By the time it cleared, she and Kurt were already on their feet and standing in front of the screen, trying to make sense of what they could see.

"Do you see them!" Kurt asked.

"Magi and Trip's suit cameras are coming back up. Trinity's is still black. Oh! She was lying on her camera. She's up, too."

"I see Dante."

Two feeds were still out. Nyx and Aria.

"No," Kurt breathed. "No, no, no. Come on, Nyx. You're tougher than that."

"Sabre, Jaguar. Bring medical supplies and meet me at the main door," Dax ordered.

She followed Kurt out of the briefing room and down the main corridor, feeling like she was in a dream. Everything felt disconnected. She hadn't just watched two people die. Had she?

"Not today," she told herself, not sure if she'd spoken the words aloud or not. "I'm not losing anyone today."

"Damn right we're not." Kurt slapped a wall panel. It slid open and a heavy first aid kit dropped to the deck. "Bring the other one." He pointed to a smaller bag still inside and then grabbed the larger and slung it over his shoulder. "Come on."

Running out of the ship was like charging into a sauna. The heat was a physical barrier that made everything harder, even breathing. They were almost to the others when a figure walked out of the smoke, her body armor shredded in places, and her blonde hair dark with soot.

Nyx. She was carrying Aria, who hung as limp as a rag doll in the cyborg's arms.

Eric yelled her name and sprinted to her. The others cried out in relief and concern. But Bobbi would remember Cris's voice later.

He uttered a strangled sound of grief and loss that lasted only a few seconds. At first, she didn't understand his reaction. Then, she saw Aria's legs. One hung at an odd angle. The other was... wrong. Flattened and twisted, her boot gone, the foot a bloody mess of flesh and bone. *Oh no.*

Kurt appeared at her side, physically turning her away from the terrible scene. He pointed her toward Trinity and the others and then sent her off with a light push. "Get them cleaned up and treated."

"Right." She hurried over to them with the first aid kit. This was something she could do. She checked them for concussions, treated their scrapes and contusions, and did her best to keep everyone's spirits up.

Dax, Nyx, and Eric joined them, and she spent some time fussing over Nyx's injuries despite the cyborg's insistence she would heal on her own.

Eric eventually stepped in. "Either she does it, or I do. But either way you're getting those looked at, so stop arguing."

None of them said anything about Aria, but every few seconds one of them would turn to look at the *Malora*. Kurt was still inside, helping Cris in whatever way he could. Bobbi had offered to donate blood, thinking her medi-bots might help, but Dax had shaken his head. Aria hadn't agreed to take the treatment yet, and he didn't want to force that decision on her.

Eventually, Dax asked the question they'd all been expecting. "What happened?"

"We should have had enough time to get out. That's why I stayed in. I was looking for the countdown mechanism. That bitch hid it, but I found it. I reset the clock."

"But there was no warning. Who kills their own people and doesn't even give them a chance to get out?" Dante asked.

"The Grays do." Nyx waved a hand to indicate the still-smoking rubble of what had been the main dome.

"Fair point," Dante agreed. "They're crazier than we thought and that's saying something."

"There was no point in sounding an alarm. None of their people were awake to hear it. She sacrificed them to try and take us out. I *fraxxed* up. I didn't realize," Eric looked over at the *Malora*, regret tightening his features. "She'll be okay. Right?"

"Trip had her stable before I left. She'll pull through." Dax's words were meant to comfort, but his tone held enough concern Bobbi knew he was holding something back. "Magi, you said you didn't realize... but you didn't elaborate. What did we miss?"

"Vivian. V.I.D.A. Whatever the hell she is. She was watching. She had to be. She waited until we were busy to activate the self-destruct so none of us noticed. It was a trap. If Sabre hadn't caught it..."

"But he did." Trinity laid a hand on Eric's shoulder.

Bobbi dropped into a crouch at his feet. "What did you see when you were inside the system?"

"V.I.D.A. Her fingerprints were all over the coding. That whole place was her design. The code, the uplinks. All of it. I found the self-destruct and reset the countdown. I couldn't deactivate it completely, but I managed to give us more time."

"And after you unplugged, the AI figured out what you'd done," she prompted him.

"Yeah. I think so. She must have done the same thing I did but in reverse. The time delay is built in. No way to override it, but she must have shortened the countdown."

"One day I am going to kill that bitch," Nyx muttered softly. "I don't know how, but it will happen."

"We'll find a way," Eric said. "And I got enough data downloaded to make a good start on finding them, including the identities of the six in those pods. One of them was Absalom. The others were a mix. I recognized a couple of names. Corporate types and scientists. Vivian must have been there as some kind of guardian."

"Good. We'll start going over everything you all found tonight. We're going to stop them, and we'll make Vivian pay for what she did to our friends," Dax said.

They lapsed into silence.

While they waited for news, Bobbi kept herself occupied thinking about the Gray Men and what they were trying to accomplish. Nova Force was fighting the ground war, but they couldn't do it alone. The Grays thought they were above the law. They were wrong. The law applied to everyone, no matter how much money and power they had. She looked around the little group and saw how tired and worried they were, the price they were paying to fight day after day. They needed new allies, and she knew where to find them. She was going to join the fight after all, just not the way she'd envisioned. The thought brought her a tiny bit of comfort as they waited to hear about Aria.

~

In his mind, Kurt knew the gravity on this world was less than standard, but his feet still felt heavy as he stepped off the ramp and onto this cursed *fraxxing* planet.

The team had stayed outside, gathered for mutual support. They all watched him approach. Only Bobbi moved, getting to her feet and walking out to meet him.

She didn't say anything. She just wrapped her arms around his waist and held him until he finally exhaled. It felt like the first time he'd taken a real breath in hours. They joined the others, his arm around her waist, holding her close and needing to feel her safe and whole beside him.

"She's out of surgery and sleeping. Trip wants to keep her under for at least another day or so to let her body heal."

Nyx looked up at him, her eyes shadowed and sad. "Her legs. I tried to protect her as best I could, but I couldn't cover all of her. How are her legs?"

"She's alive because of you. You shielded her from the worst of the blast." Kurt knew there was no easy way to say it, so he didn't try to be gentle. "Trip managed to save one leg. The other was too badly damaged. He tried everything. I don't think any doctor in the galaxy could have done more."

Not that it mattered to Cris. All he saw was his failure. Kurt had seen that in the other man's eyes. The explosion today had cost two of his teammates something precious. It was going to take time to put them both back together again.

"But she can get it replaced. Right?" Nyx asked. "She's already got a cybernetic eye."

"That's for her to decide," Dax said. "But if she wants to, then yes, that's an option."

"When she's awake, I'd like to see her. I want to apologize... and talk to her about her options," Nyx said.

"You saved her life," Kurt reminded her again.

"You're the reason she has options," Bobbi added.

"Exactly. Now she's stable, we can get the hell off this rock. Everyone back on board and hit your acceleration couch. We'll debrief once we're in orbit," Kurt said.

Dax grinned. "Are you taking over as commander?"

"No, sir. You're welcome to the job. I just want off this planet as soon as possible." The whole team had suffered a loss today. They'd won the battle, but the cost had been too high.

"Agreed."

They headed back to the ship in subdued silence. It wasn't until they were back on board he realized Bobbi didn't have a berth. "You're with me."

She gave him a tired smile. "I thought we'd established that."

"Oh, we have. But I meant you're coming with me to my quarters. My bunk doubles as an acceleration couch and it's big enough for two. If we cuddle."

"Cuddling. I like this idea."

"Then walk with me, my little minx."

Her laughter banished some of the shadows from

his mind and soothed the ragged edges of his soul. She'd fixed parts of him he hadn't known were broken.

He'd planned to have his wicked way with her once they were in bed, but the plan changed after she snuggled into his arms and uttered a contented sigh that he felt all the way down to his toes.

He shared the feeling, which surprised him. After the day they'd had, he expected to be angry, agitated, unable to settle. Instead, he felt tired but at peace. It was a good feeling—one he wanted to experience more often. All this time, he thought he had to wear himself down to keep control on his temper. He'd been wrong. What he needed was Bobbi.

He spooned behind her, one leg over hers, his nose brushing the side of her neck. "I love you."

She made another contented sound and turned her head just enough to kiss him. "I love you, too."

"Even with the nanotech, we can't know how long we'll have. But I do know this much. However long we live, whatever this *fraxxed* up universe and the Grays might throw at us. I want to share that time with you."

She nodded happily. "You. Me. And a lifetime's worth of ice cream. Sounds perfect."

EPILOGUE

CONVINCING Bobbi not to join him on this delivery run hadn't been easy. In the end, he'd had to tell her why he didn't want her there. When she'd stopped laughing, she'd agreed to stay on the *Malora*.

"You should have just said it was a guy thing."

It was more than that, but Kurt hadn't tried to explain. If he did, Bobbi might decide she wanted to come after all.

The *Minerva* was a sister to the *Malora*, which meant it was easier to dock the Bat airlock to airlock than to try and fit her into the other frigate's shuttle bay.

He made the connections and did one final walk-through, making sure everything was stored properly and the ship was as clean as the day it had been created. "Boo, it's been a pleasure."

"To you as well, Lieutenant Commander Meyer."

He paused. "She finally changed my name?"

"She did. Do you wish me to change it back?"

"No, no. That's fine." The last thing he needed was for the colonel to hear his ship call him Bossyboots.

He opened the airlock door. Archer was waiting for him. He looked different, and it took Kurt a moment to realize it was because the man was out of uniform. That would make this easier. The woman standing beside him wouldn't.

"Sir. Phylomenia. I didn't know you were on board."

The last time he'd seen Phyl, she'd been Archer's date at the gala. The fact she was here made it clear that whatever was going on between the two of them was more than just a dinner date.

"Good to see you alive and well, Kurt. I'm just here to make sure that Scott plays nice." She slapped the colonel on the ass. "Try not to be too much of an asshole, Scotty." She looked past Kurt. "Wow. Nice ship. I'll tell Garrett we're upgrading."

"Phyl!" Archer shot the woman an annoyed look. "Behave."

"We both know that is never going to happen. See you soon." She waved and walked away, leaving the two men alone.

"No sirs today. I'm here as Bobbi's uncle. How is she?" Archer stalked past him and onto the *Bat* before he turned to stare at Kurt. "What happened to her down there?"

"She killed a man with a garrote and her bare hands."

Archer flinched. "I haven't seen a report on that."

"Because she's not ready to write it."

Archer pointed to a chair and claimed the one across

from it. "Sit. I didn't think Bahl would put her in that position."

Kurt stayed standing. "Colonel Bahl used the resources she had on hand. *You* were the one who put her there."

"I pulled her off the investigation when it got too dangerous."

"The hell you did!" Kurt knew he might be kissing his career goodbye, but this needed to be said. "You dragged her into this mess, kept her involvement a secret from everyone, including the people who should have been protecting her. You let us suspect her of colluding with the enemy, for *fraxx* sake!"

"I needed to know who to trust. There was too much at stake not to take precautions."

"You used her."

Archer was back on his feet in a second. "Watch your tone, Meyer."

"You said you were here as her uncle, not my colonel. We're both off duty and out of uniform, and this is not a military vessel. You want to toss me out an airlock after this, fine. But first, I'm going to have my say. Bobbi deserved better from both versions of you, the officer and the uncle. You're her family! So why did you offer her a life-changing treatment, ban her from talking to anyone about it, even her mothers, and then leave her to inject herself with it with no one around to make sure it went right?"

"It was necessary."

"The hell it was. You wouldn't have done that to any other soldier under your command. You knew you could trust Bobbi. You also knew she'd do it for you because you're family."

Archer grimaced. "You've been talking to Phyl. Haven't you?"

"No. I came to these conclusions all on my own."

"*Fraxx*." He dropped back into his chair. "You done now? If so, sit."

This was not what Kurt had expected. He sat down. "Sir? Uh, Archer?"

"Scott. Call me Scott. I think that might be best since this is clearly an off-the-record conversation."

"Right. Si—Scott."

"You're not wrong. At least, I'm starting to realize that's a possibility. It's been brought to my attention that I've failed to protect a lot of people I care about, including my niece."

"You're not wrong," Kurt agreed.

Scott sighed and looked around at his ship. "You kept your word. You brought back my niece and my ship both in one piece. You protected her when I didn't. Thank you."

"It was my honor. Has she told you?"

"About the two of you? Yes. That's what I thought we'd be talking about. Me doing the whole protective uncle, do right by her thing." He chuckled. "I guess I got that bit wrong too."

"And you're going to help her with her plans?" Bobbi's idea was a good one. She'd seen something the rest of them hadn't—another way to take the fight to the corporations.

"The legal team specially trained to prosecute Nova

Force cases and go after the Grays? Hell, yes. Bahl is on board, too. That's going to happen. And I tracked down that Private Reddy she was asking after. And the Pheran family. All fine."

"Good. And I'm glad to hear about Reddy and the others. She was worried about them."

"She's like my sister that way. Always looking out for others."

"And she does a lot of good. We need her and this plan of hers."

"I agree. She's going to need protection, though. They're going to target her now."

"I know. I'll see to it. Anyone trying for Bobbi will have to come through me."

"That's what I needed to hear, that you'll take care of my Bobcat."

"I'm going to watch over my minx." Kurt held out his hand to Scott. "I love her, and I won't let anything happen to her."

"That is all I can ask." Scott shook his hand. "Oh, actually, there is something else."

"What do you need?"

"See if you can get Bobbi to hold off telling her mothers what happened. They're going to want to kill me when they find out I put their daughter in danger. I'll need some time to work out the right defense."

"Against a lawyer and a judge?" Kurt grinned. "Good *fraxxing* luck. Though I know an excellent lawyer…"

Kurt had planned to get shuttled back to the *Malora*. Instead, Scott ferried him over himself, flying the *Bat*. It meant that Scott and Bobbi got to have a brief reunion, with Bobbi agreeing to help smooth things over with her mothers once they learned the truth, or as much of it as they could ever be told.

Once Scott was on his way back, he and Bobbi made their way to the galley to raid the freezer.

"You two work everything out?" she asked.

"We did. Turns out we have one very important thing in common."

"You're both annoyingly bossy?"

"Okay, two things. We're bossy, and we both love you."

"I love you too." She pushed one of the bowls toward him. "Eat up. I have plans for you later. You're going to need the calories."

Kurt looked at the bowl and then at Bobbi. If this was what the rest of his life was going to look like, he was a very lucky man.

**

Thank You for Reading Operation Artemis!
Keep reading for a bonus scene teasing the next couple…

If you're looking for more stories like this one, I invite you to explore the other books in the rest of Drift universe - including the Nova Force, The Drift, and Haven Colony series.

BONUS SCENE

"I ENVY your ability to turn off your pain receptors," Aria said to Nyx. The cyborg had been a regular visitor to the med-bay, bringing her books and vids and keeping her company while she recovered. Not that she was ever really going to recover. She'd lost another piece of herself. First her eye, now her leg.

"Do you need more pain-blockers? I can call Trip," Nyx offered.

"No. Don't do that. I'm okay." And the last thing she needed was to have Cris ghosting around the med-bay. He hadn't been truly present since she'd woken up after the surgery. Dax had been the one to tell her about her leg. Cris had been there to answer questions and explain the details. He did his job and kept her comfortable, but he never tried to comfort her.

It stung more than she expected.

She'd been trying to get him to move on almost from the moment they met. He never had, and she'd gotten used to having him around. He was the friend she could turn to, a shoulder to cry on, the one who got her jokes and made her laugh no matter how lousy her day had gone.

If things had been different... She pushed the thought away. Things *were* different. Cris had finally taken her advice and moved on. All it had taken was her losing another body part. He wouldn't be the only one who wouldn't see her as human anymore. She'd deal with it. It was what she wanted. One night of hot sex before they'd learned they were on the same team had complicated everything. Now, they were finally past it.

"Have you given anymore thought to what you're going to do?" Nyx asked.

"Some. The way I see it, I've got two choices. Cash out and retire with a nice, comfy pension, or stay in, take the treatment and get the shiny cyborg leg to go with my eye. Matching set and all that."

Nyx didn't laugh. "If you retire, won't they give you a prosthetic anyway?"

"They will, but it will be the civilian model. If I stay in? They're talking about some upgrades. Things they couldn't do if I wasn't getting the medi-bot treatment, too. It won't be pleasant, but I'd be more like you when it was done."

"And you don't want that." There was no judgment in Nyx's voice.

"To be like you? You're a badass. Why wouldn't I want that? The thing is, I'm not sure I want to do this anymore." She gestured around them. "I'm tired." And she missed her friend. Team Three was her family. Always. But Cris was special. And if that was gone… Or maybe she was being stupid. Or it was the drugs in her system. Or the fact that the rest of the team had all paired up, leaving her and Cris as the only two single people left. Yeah. That was probably it.

"What would you do instead?"

That was a damned good question. "I have no *fraxxing* idea. This is all I know."

Nyx nodded. "I was the same. This is what we were made for." She patted Aria's hand, which was a surprising act of compassion from the cyborg who had never been shown any. "If you need help to adjust to your new badass self, I'll do what I can to assist."

"I haven't decided if that's what I'm going to do."

The other woman just looked at her for a long moment and then smiled. "Actually, I think you already have. I'll leave you to think for a bit. If Sabre and Jaguar have left any ice cream, do you want a bowl?"

"Two scoops, please. And check the back of the freezer, behind the blocks of algae broth."

"You hid the ice cream?"

"From Nico. That kid is an ice cream addict. I leave a carton stashed for emergencies."

"I'll be back soon. Get some rest. And I am sending Trip in to check on your medication levels. You may not want to see him right now, but he needs to see you."

She snorted. "I doubt that."

"I don't. For someone with enhanced vision, you don't see things as well as you should."

Aria's mouth opened and shut, but she couldn't

think of anything to say before Nyx vanished through the door.

Cris didn't want to see her. She'd seen that for herself. He wouldn't even look at her right now. So what was Nyx on about? What was the cyborg seeing that she couldn't? And was she taking relationship advice from someone who had killed more people than she'd kissed? "Fraxx it. I need a nap."

She'd figure it out later. After all, if she went through with the surgery, she'd have weeks of rehab and recovery ahead of her. Time was one thing she had in abundance.

***

Thank You for Reading OPERATION ARTEMIS!

I hope you enjoyed Kurt and Bobbi's story.

ABOUT THE AUTHOR

Susan lives out on the Canadian west coast surrounded by open water, dear family, and good friends. She's jumped out of perfectly good airplanes on purpose and accidentally swum with sharks on the Great Barrier Reef.

If the world ends, she plans to survive as the spunky, comedic sidekick to the heroes of the new world, because she's too damned short and out of shape to make it on her own for long.

You can find out more about Susan and her books here:
www.susanhayes.ca